"Caro," he called to her softly

"Haven't you forgotten something?"

She threw him an icy glare over her shoulder. He was twirling her glasses casually between his fingers, his blue eyes glinting provocatively.

It was all she could do not to snatch them from his grasp. She pushed the glasses back on her nose, still scowling. "Th-thank you," she stammered.

Matt studied her face with interest. "Maybe I was wrong about those glasses," he remarked. "I think I rather like them. They make you look...vulnerable."

Caro made the mistake of looking up into his eyes and as he reached out and touched her cheek she swayed unconsciously toward him.

"What I don't understand," he murmured, "is why you're so intent on disguising the fact that you're a very beautiful woman."

SUSANNE McCARTHY has spent most of her life in London, but after her marriage she and her husband moved to Shropshire. The author is now an enthusiastic advocate of this unspoiled part of England, and although she has set her novels in other locations, Susanne says that the English countryside will probably appear in many of her books.

Books by Susanne McCarthy

HARLEQUIN PRESENTS

Don't miss any of our special offers. Write to us at the following address for information on our newest releases.

Harlequin Reader Service
P.O. Box 1397, Buffalo, NY 14240
Canadian address: P.O. Box 603,
Fort Erie, Ont. L2A 5X3

SUSANNE McCARTHY

trial by love

Harlequin Books

TORONTO • NEW YORK • LONDON
AMSTERDAM • PARIS • SYDNEY • HAMBURG
STOCKHOLM • ATHENS • TOKYO • MILAN

Harlequin Presents first edition March 1991
ISBN 0-373-11348-X

Original hardcover edition published in 1989
by Mills & Boon Limited

TRIAL BY LOVE

CHAPTER ONE

THE verdict was Not Guilty. The young man in the dock hesitated, and then as relief dawned his face broke into a broad grin. A ripple of noise ran round the courtroom as the tension eased, and everyone began to fidget, waiting for the usher to announce that the court would rise.

The prosecuting barrister turned to the defence with a smile of congratulation. 'Well done,' he approved. 'That was a very neat cross-examination.

Caroline acknowledged his words with a small smile, though behind her gold-rimmed glasses her brown eyes glinted with ironic humour. Such high praise from Mr Matthew Farrar-Reid, ascendant star of the Old Bailey, when she had just made mincemeat of his case! She stood up, made her formal bow to the bench and, gathering up her books and papers, walked briskly from the court.

Matt joined her. 'I believe that's the first time you've beaten me,' he remarked lightly—but there was an unmistakable trace of arrogance in his voice. It was a justifiable arrogance, perhaps—there was no denying that Matthew Farrar-Reid was a brilliant lawyer, and he had all the ambition to take him right to the top of the tree.

Caroline had known him for nearly six years—they worked from the same set of Chambers, down in that exclusive quarter of elegant old

buildings known as the Inns of Court, between the
Royal Courts of Justice and the River Thames. But
he had barely seemed to notice her existence
before—his defeat at her hands had at last forced
him to concede her some respect!

'I ought to buy you a coffee to celebrate,' he
went on, a glint of sardonic humour in those steel-
blue eyes. 'Are you coming upstairs?'

Caroline inclined her head in dignified response.
'Thank you,' she said in a cool voice. 'I'll be up in
five minutes. I have to say goodbye to my client.'

Young Kevin Dixon was standing with his parents. Already he had removed the sober tie that
had looked so out of place beneath that ruddy
countenance, and the ebullient confidence of
youth had returned to his eyes. His father pumped
Caroline's hand with vigorous enthusiasm.

'I 'ave to admit,' he confided, 'when I found out
our brief was a woman, I told the missus, "That's
it—he's going down for a long stretch this time."
But you done 'im proud. Say thank you, then,' he
added brusquely to his son.

'Yeah, thanks, miss,' the sprig piped up enthusi-
astically. 'You was great!'

'The evidence carried the case,' she murmured
drily. Though he was certainly entitled to his
acquittal on this occasion—it was well-known, in
certain circles, that the Dixons never carried fire-
arms—it was probably fair to say that they weren't
London's most law-abiding citizens.

Mrs Dixon was studying her face closely, and
Caroline waited patiently for the inevitable question. 'Ere, Miss Kosek, I hope you don't mind me

asking, but it's your name. You ain't any relation to Adam Kosek, the actor, are you?'

'He's my father,' Caroline admitted with a certain reluctance.

'Well, I never! Oh, he's my favourite, he is! We had one of his films on the video only the other night—I can't remember what it was called, but he was a reporter, and there was this girl——'

'Oh yes, I know the one you mean,' put in Caroline quickly, hoping to stem the flow.

'You look just like him, you know—if it wasn't for them glasses. I'd never have taken him for your father, though—I wouldn't have thought he was as old as that.'

It was time to terminate this conversation! 'Well, goodbye,' she said firmly. 'And I hope I won't be seeing you again under similar circumstances.'

'Definitely not, miss,' Mr Dixon asserted firmly. 'Goodbye. And thank you again. You done a real good job—for a woman.'

Caroline reflected wryly on that parting shot as she rode up in the lift to the fourth floor. She was well used to that sort of prejudice—from clients, from instructing solicitors, from the whole 'Old Boy' structure of the legal profession.

She tried not to let it bother her. She had been warned, of course, before she had even embarked on her chosen career, that it would be difficult. But she had persevered against that dead weight of traditionalism, and over the past twelve months she had been offered better and better briefs. She was twenty-seven now, and at last she was beginning to feel that she was being taken seriously.

The price had been high. She knew that in

Chambers she was regarded as something of an Iron Maiden. With her glossy brown hair confined in a tight bun at the nape of her neck, and the severe black suit that was *de rigueur* in court, she appeared unattractive—almost gaunt.

But that was exactly the way she wanted it—crisp and businesslike, not the smallest hint of feminine frivolity. She had chosen her course—she was a career woman; she had neither the time nor the inclination for romance. But it wasn't always easy to swim against the tide, 'spinster' had such an ugly ring to it.

The lift stopped, and she walked briskly across the echoing hall and through the swing doors that led to the Bar mess. With a sigh of relief she took off her wig and bands, and slipped into the robing-room to get her handbag out of the long wooden locker where she left it while she was in court.

A swift check in her small make-up mirror confirmed that her appearance was as neat as usual, and then she hurried up the narrow stairs to the private rest-room on the top floor of the building that was reserved for the use of barristers—not even solicitors were allowed across this exclusive threshold.

It was pleasant up here. The plain electric light was restful on the eyes after the harsh fluorescent panels in the windowless court-rooms of the new wing, and the dull view of the buildings on the other side of the narrow road was obscured by spotless white net curtains. Soft beige tones and polished wood created a restful atmosphere—perfect for relaxing after the sharp battle of wits she had been engaged in downstairs.

Her erstwhile opponent, untroubled by his recent defeat, hailed her with a wave. He was seated at a table by the window with one of the other members of their Chambers, and Caroline went over to join them, grateful to avoid the queue that often accumulated at the counter at this time of day. She took her seat, smiling her thanks to Matt as he slid a cup of coffee towards her, and moving Ralph Easton's yellowing wig out of the way of a slop of tea he had spilt on the polished wooden table-top.

'Thank you, my dear,' he boomed merrily. 'So, I hear you beat young Farrar-Reid today. Jolly well done—he needs putting in his place. He's been winning far too many lately.'

'Thank you,' responded Caroline demurely. 'The evidence was in my favour.'

'A very well-prepared case,' Matt commented, leaning back lazily in his seat. 'And so another young thug is free to terrorise the streets of London.'

'If he was a thug, you should have succeeded in your prosecution,' she pointed out, regarding him with a level gaze from behind the useful defence of her thick glasses.

'Oh, yes! Jolly good!' applauded Ralph, looking to Matt to see how he would respond.

But Matthew Farrar-Reid was far too cool and self-assured to allow himself to be goaded by such paltry gibes. He merely allowed his arrogant mouth to curve into a cynical smile. 'I hope the staff of Lewisham's post offices and building societies see it in such a dispassionate light,' he remarked provocatively.

'You know as well as I do that Fred Dixon would

have had the lad's hide if he'd thought he was going out tooled up,' Caroline returned, coolly sipping her coffee.

He laughed. 'You ought to be careful,' he warned her sardonically. 'You're in danger of becoming a permanent fixture within these hallowed portals, like old Ralph here.'

'I can think of worse fates.'

'You like defending criminals?'

She returned him a cool smile. 'They aren't criminals until they've been convicted,' she pointed out, knowing he needed no lessons in professional ethics. 'And it isn't my job to decide guilt or innocence—that's for the jury.'

'You merely represent your client to the best of your ability?'

'Of course.'

'Bravo!' he applauded mockingly. 'But you really ought to broaden your horizons a little, you know. I shall have to see if I can get you in on a nice juicy prosecution one of these days.'

She acknowledged the offer with a slight inclination of her head. It could be very interesting— and she had to admit that on a professional level she would enjoy working with him; she knew she would learn a lot from him. Her reservations were entirely personal.

He was the type she didn't much care for—the type of which her father was the ultimate example. Devastatingly attractive, able to turn on the charm whenever it suited him. He was tall, with the wide shoulders and lithe frame of an athlete rather than a barrister.

His hair was light brown, almost blond, and his

eyes were steely blue—very daunting to any witness contemplating perjury. His strongly carved features bore the unmistakable stamp of a powerful intelligence, and the air of innate superiority in his bearing always commanded respect.

Which was just as well for his career, Caroline reflected wryly. If half the stories that circulated about his private life were true, they would singe the wigs of the august Masters of the Bench. He was said to have a penchant for leggy blonde models, and was highly adept at avoiding the tender trap of matrimony.

Ralph Easton levered himself wearily to his feet. 'Ah, well, back to the grindstone,' he sighed. 'I'm before the inaptly named Mr Justice Lamb for smuggling cocaine, and he does hate it if one is late back from recess.' He set his wig slightly askew on his balding head, and picking up his untidy bundle of papers hurried away down the stairs.

'Are you going back to Chambers?' Matt asked Caroline. 'I'll walk down with you.'

It was a beautiful spring day. The little cafés on the sunny side of the street opposite the Old Bailey had an almost continental air with their pavement tables and neatly trimmed bay trees, and the tulips were blooming in the brave flower-beds beside Ludgate Circus.

'Mmm, isn't it nice to see a little sunshine?' remarked Caroline with satisfaction as they strolled along. 'It's the sort of day that makes me long to be a lady of leisure.'

'Surely you could be if you wanted?' Matt asked her.

She slanted him a look of sardonic enquiry. 'Would you live off *your* father?' she countered. Sir Lionel Farrar-Reid, though now retired, had been the head of a merchant bank, and was reputed to be as rich as Croesus.

He acknowledged the point with a smile. 'No, I wouldn't,' he conceded. 'So, you decided to be an independent lady—what made you chose a career in law?'

She shrugged aside a question she had been asked many times—not least by her parents. 'Oh, it was a subject that I found fascinating,' she explained lightly. 'And I suppose I must have a dash of my father's taste for the theatrical in my blood.'

'You never thought of going on the stage yourself?'

She laughed. 'Heavens, no! One actor in the family is quite enough.'

His blue eyes smiled in response. 'And acting's a tough business if you want to get to the top,' he remarked.

'So is the law, for a woman,' she countered drily. 'We're making inroads into the lower echelons, but pushing through to the real seats of power is going to be a whole new battle.'

'You sound as if you're a feminist,' he challenged.

'That depends on what you mean exactly by "feminist".'

'Ah! A lawyer's answer,' he chided.

'But then I *am* a lawyer.'

He laughed. '*Touché*. So, what is your ambition? Do you see yourself as a High Court judge one day?'

'I wouldn't mind,' she admitted. 'But I don't think it's very likely.'

'You do have to be pretty dedicated,' he agreed. 'And for a woman, taking time out to have a family could put you right out of the running.'

'Oh, I don't think I'm very likely to do that,' she responded without thinking.

'No?' He slanted her a provocative smile. 'Having boyfriend trouble?'

Caroline felt her colour rising, and retreated into anger. 'That's really none of your business,' she countered, a little more sharply than she had intended.

His brows lifted in surprise. 'I'm sorry.'

She fought to regain her composure, embarrassed at revealing so much of herself. It was all very well for him, she reflected bitterly. No one would ever dream of asking Matthew Farrar-Reid why he had never got married. It was patently obvious that he thoroughly enjoyed his life-style.

He was rich and handsome, he drove fast cars, he had a fabulous riverside flat in a prestigious Docklands development, and when he wasn't charming juries he was conquering mountains— he had climbed the Eiger by all the most difficult routes, and a couple of years ago he had been to the Himalayas on a successful expedition to the summit of K2.

He laughed—his laugh was a soft, throaty chuckle that she couldn't deny was very attractive. 'You're right, it's none of my business,' he agreed, turning on his famous charm. 'But what do you do to relax? You must unwind somehow.'

'Oh, I swim, I play squash,' she responded, conceding a few inches of her defence.

'Really? We'll have to have a game some time— maybe I'll have better luck against you than I did this morning!'

She laughed at that. They had reached their Chambers, and Matt held the door open for her, standing back with slightly exaggerated gallantry. 'Ah,' he mocked, 'I was afraid I would bring down burning coals on my head.'

'What, for opening a door for me?' she queried.

'Certainly not. There's nothing wrong with good manners.'

'But surely in this age of equality *you* should open the door for *me*?'

'You aren't carrying an armful of books,' she pointed out with a touch of asperity.

Hugh, the bustlingly efficient Clerk of Chambers, glanced up as they came in. 'Ah, Caroline. You're Defrauding Customs and Excise at the Inner London Sessions tomorrow,' he told her. 'Judge Lane presiding.'

'Oh, you'll be all right with him,' commented Matt, deliberately seeking to provoke her. 'Just give him your sweetest smile and he'll award you special costs.'

She favoured him with a frosty glare as she moved over to see what was waiting on the mantelpiece for her. 'You've got Barney Watson against you,' Hugh added.

'Don't let him mutter while you're talking,' Matt advised her. 'It's a very bad habit of his.'

'Thank you,' she responded drily, forbearing to mention that she was well aware of Barney's irritating quirk. 'Heavens!—a cheque! Wonders will never cease!'

'Ah crime pays, but only slowly,' said Matt, opening two cheques of his own.

'Which doesn't matter a scrap to you, because you don't need the money,' put in Sir Arthur, the head of Chambers, as he strolled into the room. 'Is that silver monster parked in the quad another one of yours?'

'If you mean the Lagonda, yes, it is. A real beauty, isn't she?'

Sir Arthur lifted his eyes to heaven in mock despair. 'I won't ask you how much it drinks in petrol!'

Matt laughed. 'Ah, you don't take a princess out to dinner and feed her fish and chips,' he pointed out drily.

Caroline bristled at the supreme male arrogance in his voice. She scooped up her books and swept out of the room with towering dignity—though she doubted if he would even notice.

She had the smallest room in Chambers, tucked away at the top of the tall building, but the small dormer window looked out over Temple Gardens and the row of grey warships moored alongside the Embankment. And at least she usually had it to herself—her co-tenant spent most of his days sitting as a Recorder.

She took her gown out of her blue bag and hung it on a hanger, and sat down at her desk. But somehow she couldn't concentrate on her work this afternoon. Restlessly she got up and strolled

over to the window, and stood gazing down at the
trees, just breaking into leaf along the river-bank.

It was nearly six years since she had arrived
here, fresh from university, to be Sir Arthur's
pupil. Even then, Matt Farrar-Reid had been
tipped as a high-flier. In those days she had been
lucky to get so much as a curt 'good morning' from
him, and she had told herself that it was a waste
of time to let herself indulge in stupid romantic
fantasies about him. She had kept very strictly to
that resolution ever since. Just because he had
been unusually friendly today. . .

The buzz of the telephone cut insistently across
her thoughts. It was Hugh. 'Ah, Caroline—I've
got Simpson junior on the line to instruct you in
Grievous Bodily Harm,' he informed her in his
idiosyncratic clipped fashion.

'Thank you, Hugh. Put him on.' She turned her
back on the gardens and the river. This was the
serious business of the law, and she gave it her
full attention.

On Sunday, as usual, she drove down to have
lunch with her mother, but when she arrived at
the riverside house she was surprised to find her
father there. She cast him a frosty glance. 'Hello.
What are you doing here?' she inquired drily.

His liquid brown eyes—those eyes that still
induced casting directors to see him as a romantic
lead though he was well into his fifties—reflected
a finely tuned blend of hurt and surprise. 'But I
live here,' he reminded her.

'Good heavens, do you really?' countered
Caroline, her voice sharp with sarcasm. 'I'd better

get my eyes tested again—I must need stronger glasses.'

'Really, Caroline! Sometimes you do let your sense of humour go just a little over the top,' he protested.

'I need a sense of humour with you for a father,' she retaliated. 'So what brings you home, anyway? Has your latest girlfriend gone back to school to take her O levels?'

'Oh, Caroline, *please*!' her mother wailed. 'Don't start an argument, not today.'

Caroline regarded her mother with wry pity. It was difficult to imagine that this thin, anxious woman had once been a stunning beauty. She had been a dancer until Adam Kosek had walked into her life, sweeping her off her feet, making her pregnant and marrying her within the space of three months. She had given up her career at his behest, and spent the rest of her life living in his shadow and making excuses for his reprehensible behaviour.

Caroline had learned early that the reality of her parents' marriage was very different from the illusion that her father liked to foster for the benefit of the media. But she had learned too that her mother was defenceless against him, and so she still allowed herself to be part of the farce that was their lives.

'All right,' she conceded patiently. 'Just tell me why you're here.'

He bestowed on her his best paternal smile, and took her hand, drawing her down to sit beside him on the big sofa. 'Listen, my dear,' he began, his

voice deep with sincerity, 'you know your mother
and I have had our difficulties over the years. . .'

She drew her hand firmly from his. 'The cameras
aren't rolling now, Dad,' she reminded him tartly.
'Just the plain version will do.'

'The plain version is that we're going to give it
another try. You don't throw away thirty good
years of marriage over one little misunder-
standing.'

'Miss Who?'

He smiled fondly at her. 'I know you've been
very upset about it all,' he went on. 'But I'm going
to make it up to you—I promise.'

'Oh, yes? What are you going to do? Buy me a
giant teddy-bear? Or a pony, maybe? I'm not
eleven years old any more, Dad. I can see through
you like a pane of glass. You'll promise Mum the
moon while it suits you, and five minutes later
you'll be off chasing some piece of skirt young
enough to be your granddaughter!'

'Now, Caro, that's enough!' he snapped,
abruptly switching to a different script. 'You're
upsetting your mother.'

'*I'm* upsetting her? Who didn't even bother to
phone on her birthday? Not so much as a bunch
of flowers!'

'That's all in the past,' her mother insisted,
dabbing at her eyes with a damp handkerchief.
'This time it really is going to be different.'

Caroline sighed. 'Oh, Mum! How often has he
promised you that?'

'But this time I know he means it.' She cast her
husband a radiant glance, and he returned his

warmest smile—the one that had melted the leading lady's heart in *Forget Not my Lovely*.

'All right. Well, we'll wait and see, then, shall we?' Caroline conceded tersely. 'I'm going to see Maggie in the kitchen. Er. . .you will still be here when I get back, won't you, Dad? I'm likely to be at least twenty minutes—do you think this romantic reconciliation can last that long?'

He smiled benevolently—Dr Seymour from *Just Before Dawn*. 'You and your little jokes! You run along now—I've a nice surprise for you, but I'll tell you about it after lunch.'

Caroline escaped gratefully to the kitchen, where Maggie was busy at the cooker, magicking-up her delicious home-made minestrone. She glanced up from her work as Caroline entered the room, and smiled. 'What's wrong?'

Caroline sighed as she sat down. 'Why doesn't she ever learn?' she demanded impatiently. 'How many times has he done this to her? And every time she falls for it, those same old lines!'

'She loves him,' Maggie explained with the tolerance of one who had watched the repetitive soap opera that was the Kosek household for the past twenty-five years.

'Huh! Well, if that's what love does to you, I'm glad I'm never likely to risk catching it!'

Maggie's expression softened. 'Ah, you will one day,' she said in a voice that was meant to be reassuring. 'One day you'll meet someone special, and right away you'll know he's the one.'

'No, thank you,' responded Caroline, reaching out to steal a flapjack from the wire cooling-tray. 'I'm going to die an old maid.'

Maggie shook her head sadly. 'Don't say that—you're much too pretty for that.'

'Maggie, I *like* being an old maid,' she insisted. 'I'm twenty-seven years old, I have a career I love, plenty of friends, plenty of money, a nice flat—what more could I ask of life?' If there was the faintest tremor of uncertainty in her voice, she suppressed it ruthlessly. 'I'm completely independent, not answerable to anyone. I'd be an absolute idiot to give all that up just because I managed to fool myself into believing I was in love with someone.'

'Don't you believe in love?'

'No, I do not,' she declared resolutely. 'It's just something that was made up by the film industry. It doesn't exist outside the sort of rubbishy tearjerkers my father stars in.'

'Oh, you don't mean that,' asserted Maggie with a comfortable smile. 'Anyway let's get this lunch served, shall we?' she added, bringing the saucepan to the table to pour the appetising contents into a fine china tureen. 'Can you carry the soup-bowls in for me?'

Caroline didn't find it easy to keep her temper during lunch. Somehow it now appeared that all the problems in the marriage had been entirely her mother's fault—but her father had very generously forgiven her, for which she was duly grateful.

'I think a nice bottle of that Chablis would go down well right now,' he suggested as Maggie brought in the main course. 'Is there any left, Maggie?'

'Aye, there's a couple of bottles in the pantry,' the housekeeper told him, pretending to grump.

Adam rose at once to his feet, and squeezed her shoulders affectionately as he passed behind her. 'I'll get it,' he murmured with cozening warmth. 'You don't have to keep running up and down.'

Maggie feigned to ignore him, and carried on serving up the vegetables. Adam returned a moment later with a chill-dewed bottle of the expensive wine.

'Here we are,' he announced proudly, pouring the wine with a flourish. 'Now, my darling Betty, I drink to you.' He lifted his wine glass, and chinked it against hers. 'My one and only love.'

'Yeuk!' Caroline pulled a face. 'Don't tell me, let me guess—*Moondance*? No, it's got to be from *Gemini Rising*—the scene where Lord Duncan finds Marianne in Sardinia.'

Her father glared at her, and her mother looked upset. 'Oh, Caroline, please,' she begged. 'Don't spoil everything, not now.'

'But how could I spoil it?' she enquired artlessly. 'This time it's the real thing, isn't it?'

'Yes, but. . .Oh, I hope you won't behave like this next Saturday!'

'Oh?' Caroline turned to her father with a glance of cool enquiry.

A flicker of annoyance crossed his face. He clearly hadn't intended to let the cat out of the bag just yet. 'The Academy are giving a dinner for your uncle Ted,' he explained reluctantly.

'Ah, so that's it! So it's time for the Perfect Family to be taken out of the closet and dusted down. I guessed it was something like that.'

'Oh, Caroline. . .'

'Don't wring your hands, mother,' Caroline begged caustically. 'You don't have to worry. I'll be there on my little chalk mark when the cameras start to roll, and I'll remember all my lines. Don't I always?'

'I hope you won't wear those awful glasses this time,' her father added.

'Yes, dear, and do try to do something nice with your hair. It looks so pretty when you make an effort.'

'You wouldn't like to pick which dress I should wear, would you?'

'Oh, no, dear. I know you'll pick something nice.' Her mother smiled complacently.

Caroline sighed. 'Here we go again,' she told herself bitterly. It was no wonder she had such an aversion to the game of love!

CHAPTER TWO

'Well, will I do?' Caroline's tone was rich with sarcasm as she twirled to show herself off to her father. Sometimes on these occasions she obstinately stuck to the severely plain image she chose for work, but at other times she would amuse herself by dressing to kill.

Her dress was a vibrant shade of coral pink that flattered her colouring and would draw every eye. It was styled with elegant simplicity, emphasising her graceful height. Her hair was her one vanity— a rich mahogany brown, it fell dead straight and glossy to below her waist. She had left it loose, catching it back from her temples with tortoiseshell combs to emphasise the fine bones of her face. And she had left off her glasses.

Her mother was warmly approving. 'Oh, you *do* look nice!' she enthused, glancing eagerly at her husband for confirmation. 'Doesn't she, Adam?'

'Absolutely lovely,' Adam Kosek agreed. 'Why can't you make an effort like that all the time?'

Caroline's eyes kindled, and her mother intervened quickly. 'I think the car's here. Come along, we don't want to be late,' she urged brightly.

The elegant white Rolls-Royce purred along in the steady stream of traffic heading into the West End for a Saturday night out. Turning into Park Lane, it drew to a stately halt outside one of London's top hotels. A small crowd had gathered, penned back behind red silk ropes, to watch the stars arrive. It was a glittering evening.

Flash-bulbs exploded as Adam Kosek stepped from his car with his wife and daughter, and several of the women cried out in excitement at the sight of him. He gave them one of his best smiles, pausing to sign a few autographs, and then swept on into the smart foyer, a lady on each arm.

This was the sort of evening that Caroline loathed—all dazzle and show, insincere smiles and the sort of small talk that she was no good at. If it wasn't for her mother, she would never come to such occasions, but she couldn't leave poor Betty to cope alone with Adam's unpredictable behaviour.

Fortunately she wasn't really expected to participate—it was enough for her to stand by her father's side, gracefully erect, an enigmatic smile curving her mouth. The faces around her were no more than a fairground pageant, anyone more than ten feet away from her was just a blur of features.

But suddenly in the midst of that amorphous throng her eyes were caught by a familiar profile, a familiar movement. She had to look a second time to be sure, and at that moment he turned towards her, and smiled in surprised recognition. He spoke a quick word to his companion, and then he was easing his way through the crowd towards her.

'Caroline! I hardly recognised you—you *do* look different.'

'So I should hope,' she answered drily. 'This is hardly the sort of thing I'd wear in court.'

'Even so. . .' Those cool blue eyes surveyed her with undisguised approval. 'The transformation is quite startling.'

She shifted uncomfortably. What an unfortunate coincidence that he should be here—she usually preferred to keep this side of her life quite separate from her work. But politeness dictated that she obey the social conventions, so reluctantly she made the essential introductions.

'Mother, this is a colleague of mine—Matthew Farrar-Reid. Matt—my mother.'

He took the pale hand held out to him, and shook it politely. 'I'm very pleased to meet you, Mrs Kosek,' he said, that deep, attractive voice that carried so much weight in a courtroom winning from Caroline's mother a sudden admiring smile.

'Matthew?' She turned to Caroline, still firmly holding on to his strong fingers. 'You've never mentioned a Matthew,' she accused.

There was a trace of sardonic humour in those steely eyes. 'We've shared Chambers for—oh, about six years, isn't it, Caroline?'

'Really?' Betty Kosek looked amazed that anyone could have worked around such a marvellous man for so long without telling her mother all about him. He certainly looked attractive tonight, even in such élite company. His black dinner-jacket was elegantly cut to mould his wide shoulders, but he wore it with the same casual panache as he wore his oddly archaic wig and gown in court.

'I'm trying to coax your daughter into coming over to the side of the Crown,' he went on smoothly. 'I'm afraid she's spending too much time haunting the cells of Brixton and the Scrubs.'

Betty had let go of his hand, but now had a firm hold on his arm instead. 'I quite agree,' she confided. 'All those nasty criminals! I'm sure I'd be much happier if she gave it up. The side of the Crown, did you say? Now that sounds much nicer.'

Caroline smiled wryly. Any connection with Royalty would always appeal to her mother, even if she had little idea what Matt was talking about.

'By the way, have you met my husband?' Betty added, giving Adam's arm a sharp tug to draw his attention away from a pneumatic blonde who was giggling up at him. 'Adam, this is a friend of Caroline's,' she told him, her voice warning him that she would not tolerate him showing her up by flirting with someone else in front of their friends. 'Matthew. . .er. . .Farrar-Reid, wasn't it?'

Adam Kosek slipped easily into the role of patrician, offering Matt his hand. 'Good evening, young man. Nice to meet you,' he greeted him with gracious condescension.

'And you, sir.'

Caroline winced. Those shrewd blue eyes were expert at spotting a phoney—it would take him about three seconds to sum up her father.

'So you're a friend of my daughter's?'

'Matthew works with Caroline, dear,' his wife put in.

'Really? You're not a thespian then?' There was a tinge of relief in his voice—clearly he had already realised that the younger man could be a strong contender for the kind of roles he played himself.

'But then I always say that the two professions are very much akin. Don't you agree? You have the courtroom for your stage, the jury for your critics. Though yours is a much nobler profession, I have no doubt.'

'Oh, I wouldn't necessarily say that,' Matt responded, an inflection of sardonic humour in his voice.

Adam looked slightly ruffled, suspecting that this facetious young man didn't quite appreciate as he should the singular honour of conversing with the Great Actor. 'Ah! It looks as if it's time to go in to dinner,' he announced, grasping the diversion with relief. 'Come along, my dear.' He took Caroline's arm, nodded a lofty farewell to Matt, and sailed into the grand dining-room.

A long table had been set up on a raised dais, where the guest of honour and his closest associates were to sit. Adam Kosek and his family, of course, were numbered among these, and Caroline took her place with a sinking heart. She hated to be put on show in this way—the perfect family, for the benefit of the cameras that were waiting to record the highlights of the evening.

It was a sumptuous banquet that had been laid on. Course followed course in a lavish display of luxury, and then the speeches began, each outdoing the last in sycophantic eloquence. Caroline stifled a yawn, trying hard to look as if she was enjoying herself.

She scanned the tables short-sightedly, and found Matt. He was with an exotic-looking dark-skinned girl. Caroline recognised her as one of the stars of a current television detective series—

though she looked very different in her stunning evening dress, her hair elaborately plaited and beaded, her high cheekbones emphasised with a wing of gold gloss. He was leaning close to her, laughing at something she was saying. At least someone was having a good time, she reflected acidly.

Yes, there was no denying that he was a very attractive man, she mused, watching him covertly. The sort of man that script-writers loved to invent—smooth and urbane in his well-cut dinner-jacket, but still with that underlying hint of raw masculinity. She could just imagine him in heavy climbing gear, scaling some treacherous rock-face.

At last the speeches were coming to an end, toasts were being drunk, and Uncle Ted had risen to make his response. And then at last the bright arc-lights that had been necessary for the television cameras were turned off. Dinner-jackets were removed as the guests relaxed; quite a few began to drift out to the hotel's bar.

'Well, I think that went off pretty well, don't you?' mused Adam with smug satisfaction, leaning back in his seat and draining his brandy-glass. Caroline smiled. Her mother was looking pleased and happy, so maybe the evening had been worth while after all. 'Why don't we go and have a little nightcap in the bar before we leave?' he suggested genially.

The bar was crowded, but Adam Kosek made a grand entrance. He naturally knew most of the people there, and of course he had to linger and exchange a few words with them all. The 'little nightcap' extended to three or four drinks, then more. His voice was getting louder, his face redder, as the evening wore on.

Across the room, Caroline saw Matt watching, and there was no mistaking the sardonic twist of his mouth. She tilted her head at a proud angle. Why should she care what he thought? It was just a nuisance that he was here. Not that anyone could accuse Matt Farrar-Reid of being a gossip— but he really was the last person she would have wanted to witness her father's embarrassing behaviour. She had always felt at a disadvantage around him, and now it would be worse.

Adam was getting drunker and drunker. It was inevitable that it would end in disaster, and it did. There was a film director there whom he had long despised, as drunk as he. Voices were raised, there was a scuffle, and Adam crashed to the floor, taking several of the nearest tables with him.

'Adam! Oh, my goodness!' Betty was thrown into a panic, and between trying to calm her and trying to check that her father hadn't injured himself in his fall Caroline felt helpless.

But suddenly there was a calm, capable presence there, taking over. 'Mrs Kosek, may I be of some assistance?'

Caroline glanced up from the floor, where she was kneeling beside her father, to see her mother fluttering gratefully around Matt. 'Oh, indeed! So kind of you. I really don't know. . .It's his blood pressure, you see. Sometimes he gets these giddy turns.'

Matt's lips twitched as he repressed a smile. 'Of course,' he agreed solemnly. He bent to the body on the floor. 'Mr Kosek, can you get up?' he coaxed.

Adam snorted derisively, but he seemed to have entirely forgotten his recent argument. With Matt's strong arm beneath his shoulder, and Caroline supporting him on the other side, he was able to struggle unsteadily to his feet.

'We're going home,' Matt explained to him in a voice firm enough to penetrate the brandy fog in his brain.

'What? Oh. . .yes, of course,' he agreed blearily, somehow managing to put one foot in front of the other.

Fortunately most of the Press photographers had left, and none of those that were left felt inclined to waste any film on pictures of Adam Kosek the worse for drink—it would hardly be a scoop. A taxi was waiting at the kerb as they coaxed Adam down the front steps, and Matt helped him on to the back seat, where he sprawled out and began to snore loudly.

Matt laughed wryly as he tried to prop him up, and Caroline glared at them both as she took her seat opposite. She was furious with her father for putting her in the position of having to be grateful to Matthew Farrar-Reid and angry with Matt if he should be feeling sorry for her.

'Really, this is so very kind,' Betty repeated as the taxi pulled away from the kerb. 'I don't know what we would have done without you.'

'I'm glad that I was there to help,' he assured her politely.

Caroline's eyes glittered in the darkness. 'What happened to your girlfriend?' she asked him.

'I sent her home in a taxi. She quite understood the circumstances.'

'How very generous of her,' she muttered bitterly under her breath, and turned to stare fixedly out of the window at the passing streets. She didn't say another word for the whole journey, leaving it in her mother's capable hands to maintain a flow of inane conversation to which, to his credit, Matt managed to respond with a semblance of interest.

Her parents' house was set in a large, leafy garden. The taxi drew up outside, and Matt helped Adam out of it. One breath of the cool night air was one breath too many, and Adam had to be virtually carried up the rose-bordered path to the front door, with his wife solicitously in attendance.

'Won't you stay and have a coffee, Matthew?' Betty invited pleadingly, turning on him her sweetest smile. 'You must let me thank you properly for everything you've done.'

'It was no trouble,' he assured her again. 'But I would certainly appreciate a coffee.'

Caroline shot him a fulminating glare, but he merely returned her a bland smile. 'I'd better tell the taxi to go, then,' she suggested pointedly, but she was already talking to the back of his head as he assisted her father carefully across the hall to the stairs.

She paid off the taxi, and went into the house. Maggie, in dressing-gown and slippers, had got up to help put Adam to bed—it seemed that a fourth assistant would be quite superfluous, so Caroline went into the drawing-room. For once,

she felt like having a brandy herself, to help soothe
her taut nerves.

She turned sharply as Matt came into the room.
'Could I trade that coffee for a shot of something
stronger?' he asked pleasantly, glancing at the cut-
glass decanter in her hand.

She smiled thinly. 'You need one too?' she
asked, pouring him one and pouring herself a
second. She lifted her dark eyes expressively
towards the upstairs room where her father was
being put to bed. 'Welcome to the happy home-
stead,' she remarked acidly, holding up her glass
in a toast and draining it in one swallow.

He put a restraining hand on her wrist as she
moved to pour herself another. 'That's your third,'
he reminded her gently. 'It won't help if you get
drunk too.'

'It'll help me,' she sighed, but she put the
decanter down without refilling her glass. 'It goes
without saying, of course, that I'd be more than
grateful if you'd forget all about tonight?' she
added with difficulty.

He smiled sympathetically. 'Of course.'

Suddenly she was aware that her heart was
beating rather too fast. The reaction surprised
her—she had thought she had learned enough
self-discipline to control that sort of thing. Carefully she moved away from him to sit down in one
of the armchairs.

Matt came over to sit opposite her, quite relaxed,
seeming to exude an aura of sophistication and
charm without the least conscious effort. 'I gather
this sort of thing has happened before?' he
remarked.

'Oh, frequently. If he doesn't get drunk and call someone out, he goes off after some twinkling starlet and we don't see him for weeks on end.'

'Why does your mother put up with him?'

She shrugged. 'Oh, I think she's rather fond of being the one woman that Adam Kosek married,' she mused with weary cynicism. 'It gives her some kind of status. Besides, think how dull life would be for her without all this melodrama.'

'You sound bitter.'

'Not in the least,' she countered, her eyes glittering defensively. 'I'm a big girl now—I've made a life of my own.'

'But it's still affecting you,' he insisted.

'Oh, cut the psychological analysis,' she returned with a snap, getting up impatiently and going back to the sideboard. Without thinking she began to pour herself another drink, but he came up behind her and took the decanter out of her hand.

'You'll turn into a alcoholic if you're not careful,' he warned firmly.

Her eyes blazed. 'Damn you, will you mind your own business?' she hissed. 'I'm not an alcoholic—in fact I very rarely drink at all. It's just. . .tonight I need it.'

He shook his head. 'That *is* the way to dependence,' he reminded her, a slow smile curving that arrogant mouth. 'I know a better way to help you relax.'

Slowly he lifted her hand, and put his lips to the hectic pulse that fluttered inside her wrist. She stared up at him, mesmerised by the deep, deep blue of his eyes. It was a situation that was totally unexpected, and she had no idea how to handle it.

What could have happened she didn't care to guess, but to her relief at that moment she heard her mother and Maggie coming down the stairs. She drew away from him sharply, struggling to regain some semblance of control, afraid her mother might sense that there was something wrong.

'Ah, Matthew!' Betty came forward, holding out both hands to him. 'I really don't know how to thank you. My husband is feeling a little better now.' She gave a tinkling laugh. 'The doctor has warned him so often against overdoing it, but— oh, you men! You never will admit when you're ill.'

Caroline suppressed a weary sigh. Her mother had spent nearly thirty years rewriting reality— she wasn't going to face up to it now.

'Ah, Maggie—the coffee. Thank you so much. Milk and sugar, Matthew?'

'Black, no sugar, thank you,' he responded, making himself confortable on one of the settees.

'You really must allow me to thank you properly,' she twittered on. 'Perhaps Caro could bring you to dinner one evening.'

'That would be very nice,' he agreed, a glint of amusement in his eyes as he noted Caroline's marked lack of enthusiasm.

'Lovely! Now that's a promise,' she warned him archly. 'Don't forget now, Caroline—I'm leaving it to you to arrange. I'm going to be looking forward to it.'

Caroline suppressed a sigh. Betty had an unfortunate habit of indulging in this sort of clumsy matchmaking on her daughter's behalf. It was most embarrassing, but it was useless to remonstrate with her—then she would be subjected to endless reproaches for her failure to find herself a husband and provide her mother with a much wanted grandchild to dote on.

But she was *not* going to sit here and let herself be made a fool of in front of Matt Farrar-Reid. 'I think I'll go up to bed,' she announced bluntly. She slanted Matt her most saccharine smile. 'Goodnight.'

Betty looked disappointed. 'Oh, but you haven't drunk your coffee yet,' she protested.

'I don't want it—caffeine keeps me awake.'

'Oh. Well. . .goodnight then, Caro, dear.' Making the best of it, Betty squeezed her hand with a show of affection. 'Sleep well.'

'Goodnight,' added Matt, rising to his feet.

Caroline hesitated, unsure of herself. His manner was impeccably polite, yet somehow she couldn't rid herself of the conviction that he was mocking her. She returned him an icy glare, which he met with a bland smile. Confused, she turned away and hurried up to her room.

By Monday morning Caroline had regained her normal composure, and her step was brisk as she walked up the path to her Chambers. It was pouring with rain, and the worn pavement was awash with puddles. The dark Gothic buildings towered against the grey sky, their windows glowing with warm light, and the gnarled old plane tree in Middle Temple Lane was dripping and bedraggled.

She stepped into the shelter of the dusty porch, where her own name was proudly listed in black letters on a strip of white-painted wood, second from the bottom now, but not yet as comfortably faded as those higher up the row. Lowering her umbrella, she shook it vigorously as she released the catch, and drew a cry of protest from someone who was just approaching.

'Hey, careful with that! You're drowning me!'

She had just a fraction of a second to catch her breath before she found herself looking up into Matt's blue eyes. 'Oh. . .I'm sorry—I didn't see you,' she gasped.

'I'm not surprised—you were walking along in a dream.' He stepped into the porch beside her, and shook out his own umbrella. 'How are you?' he asked.

The tone of his voice told her that it was meant to be more than just a general Monday-morning enquiry, and she felt an uncomfortable twist of embarrassment, but she tilted up her chin at a proud angle. 'I'm fine,' she asserted coolly.

'And your father?'

'He's very well, thank you.'

'Recovered from his. . .er. . .giddy turn?'

Her eyes flashed him a frost warning. 'Perfectly recovered, thank you,' she bit out, and, turning him an aloof shoulder, she hurried into the cluttered warmth of Hugh's tiny office.

Nearly everyone was there, grumbling about the weather and the long delays in receiving legal-aid cheques. 'I'm sick of crime,' Ralph Easton was complaining as usual. 'Why can't the Lord Chancellor tip me the wink, like lucky old Latimer?'

'You don't play golf with the right judges,' Matt told him genially, following Caroline into the room. 'You'll never get called to the bench. If you're not careful you'll be slumming it down the Bailey for the rest of your days.'

'It's all right for you to talk,' complained Ralph, waving the pink-ribboned brief he had taken from the mantelpiece. 'There's no danger of you getting fobbed off with a three-handed take-and-drive-away down at Kingston Crown Court. Another not-guilty spieler, I suppose.'

Matt laughed. 'I've got a very interesting Murder on my hands,' he said to Caroline. 'Would you like to take a look at it?'

She hesitated for a fraction of a second. If it had been any other morning. . .'I'm afraid I don't really have time at present,' she temporised. 'I've a couple of briefs in the Court of Appeal, and I gather there's a trial collapsed in number seven court, so my Aggravated Burglary's likely to be coming off this morning.'

'I see.' He stood aside to let her pass through the door, but as she climbed the narrow stairs to her office on the top floor he came after her. 'Caroline. . .?' She paused, and half turned towards him, one eyebrow raised in indifferent enquiry. 'Is there something wrong?' he asked. 'Have I done something to annoy you?'

'On the contrary,' she responded stiffly. 'You've given me every reason to be grateful to you.'

'Ah!' A glint of amusement lit the steel-blue of his eyes. 'And you don't like that, do you?'

Damn him, why did he have to be so perceptive? It was as if he could read every thought that was racing through her brain.

He turned on that irresistibly charming smile. 'I could give you the chance to thank me properly,' he suggested smoothly. 'The Barbican Theatre are doing a season of Oscar Wilde. Would you like to come with me one evening?'

'No, thank you.'

She had spoken a little too sharply, and anger flickered in the blue depths of his eyes. But it was instantly controlled. 'The ballet, then?' he enquired blandly. 'Or is your taste for the avant-garde?'

Caroline returned him a cool, level gaze. 'What's happened to the girl you were with the other night?' she enquired, instilling a note of icy sarcasm into her voice. 'Did she object after all to being unceremoniously bundled off in a taxi on her own?'

He smiled slowly. 'Vanessa's just a friend.'

'Is she really? A very *good* friend, I suppose?'

'You mean in the journalistic sense?'

'I don't mean in any sense at all,' she countered with icy disdain. 'I really couldn't care less. And I have no wish to have my name in your little black book either.' She turned away, hating the sound of his sardonic laughter.

'Your mother wants you to take me home for dinner,' he reminded her provocatively.

'Oh, she'll soon forget about it,' Caroline retorted. 'She always does.'

He was still laughing as he strolled into his office, and as she climbed the stairs to her own door she heard him pick up the phone. Whoever he was calling didn't take long to answer, and when he spoke his voice held a note of warm intimacy that made Caroline stiffen.

'Hello, darling. . .Yes, of course it's me—didn't I promise you I'd call? Listen, what are you doing tonight? The Barbican Theatre are doing a season of Oscar Wilde. . .Good. I'll pick you up at six— we can have dinner first.'

Suddenly Caroline realised with a shock of horror that she was actually eavesdropping! Appalled, she stepped quickly into her own office, closing the door firmly behind her. She dumped her bag on the floor and took off her coat, and sat down at her desk.

Her hands were shaking. Dammit, she shouldn't let him get under her skin like this. It was unfortunate that what had happened over the weekend had disturbed the usual pattern of their relationship. But at least she could retain some dignity in the situation.

Matt was dangerous—she had told herself that a long time ago. Behind that cool, faintly sardonic façade there lay a hard core of uncompromising maleness that drew an instinctive response from almost every woman he met. She would have to be careful—but if she behaved with the utmost decorum he would soon forget that he had ever seen her as anything other than the unattractive Miss Kosek, spinster career woman.

CHAPTER THREE

THE Mediterranean sun was gloriously hot. Caroline lay back on a sun-lounger, her eyes closed behind her sun-glasses. At least she could get a tan while she was here—though the annual junket of the Cannes Film Festival was not exactly her idea of the perfect holiday.

Most people would envy her, she reflected wryly, staying at one of the Riviera's most luxurious hotels, surrounded by dozens of the most handsome heroes of the silver screen. But she was bored stiff— the level of conversation had yet to rise above who- was-sleeping-with-who and who-was-going-to- star-in-whose-next-smash-hit-movie.

One of her father's films was featuring promi- nently this year—his face was everywhere, on dozens of fly-posters along the boulevard, on hoardings twenty feet high. She and her mother had been dragged along to co-star in their usual roles of devoted, happy family.

Caroline opened one jaded eye and glanced around. The beach was draped with beautiful bodies, most of them—like herself—wearing only the briefest of bikini bottoms. Few of the women present were over thirty—by that age, if they hadn't been traded in for a younger model, they usually passed their time spending their husbands' money in the shops of Nice or Cannes, or losing it in the casino in the glittering modern Palais des Festivals.

She was about to close her eyes again when she saw her mother on the wooden steps that climbed down to the beach from the white-railed boulevard above. She had someone with her. Caroline squinted shortsightedly, trying to see. There was something familiar about that tall figure. Oh, no! What on earth was Matt Farrar-Reid doing here? Hadn't he gone off climbing somewhere?

But here he was, walking across the beach towards her, his blue eyes surveying every inch of her honey-tanned body with undisguised appreciation. She felt her heart begin to race alarmingly. She was furious—he was blatantly ignoring the informal rule of etiquette that dictated that a man should not stare too openly at a woman when she was sunbathing.

But she couldn't reach for her T-shirt to cover herself without giving him the satisfaction of knowing she was embarrassed. She could only sit there, acutely conscious of the ripe swell of her naked breasts, pertly tipped with rosebud pink, as he let his gaze linger there for one insolent moment too long.

The warmth of a blush was spreading right through her body as she struggled to control her ragged breathing. 'H. . .hello,' she managed to say, her voice taut with the effort of keeping it steady. 'What are you doing here?'

He smiled in mocking amusement. 'That's not a very warm welcome!'

'Wasn't it a coincidence?' her mother put in

eagerly. 'There I was, just doing a little window-shopping in town, when who should I see at one of those nice little pavement cafés?' She squeezed his arm, as affectionately as if he were her oldest friend.

'Oh? I thought you'd be halfway up a mountain by now,' remarked Caroline, intentionally draining any shade of interest from her voice.

'I was,' he answered, quite untroubled by her indifference. 'But my cousin Mike got an urgent message from home—some impending business disaster. End of climb. I suppose I could have stayed on and joined up with another party, but I'm not very keen on climbing with total strangers. So I thought I'd come and soak up a little sun instead.'

'Matthew's checked into our hotel,' her mother put in. 'It was most fortunate—everywhere's so crowded. But I had a little word with the manager, and it was soon fixed. Well, now, I'm sure you two have lots to talk about, so you won't miss me. I'm meeting your father for lunch, Caro, dear.'

She fluttered away, and Matt sat down in the sand beside Caroline. She couldn't help noticing that a number of the sleek beauties lying around on the beach were showing a considerable interest in him. She smiled wryly to herself.

'This is the life,' he remarked lazily, letting his eyes rove appreciatively over the scenery, returning some of the inviting smiles that were being cast his way.

'It isn't considered polite to stare,' she reminded him with a touch of asperity.

'I'm sorry.' His blue eyes glinted with sardonic

amusement, and she returned him a frosty glare. If he thought she was *jealous*——! As casually as she could, she reached for her T-shirt and pulled it on over her head. Now she felt a little less vulnerable.

'Aren't you sunbathing any more?' he taunted.

'I don't like to overdo it,' she responded coolly. 'Too much sun can age the skin.'

'Really? It didn't look to me as if you had any need to be concerned.'

Her eyes flashed him an explicit warning, but his smile was unabashed. He leaned back in the warm sand, folding his hands behind his head and closing his eyes. Caroline found herself staring at him, suddenly very aware of the raw maleness of his body.

He was wearing khaki-coloured trousers of tough drill cotton, and a sleeveless dark green T-shirt. The muscles in his arms were smooth and powerful beneath bronzed skin, his hair was streaked blond by the sun in the mountains. She looked away sharply, her mouth dry.

'Have you had some good climbing?' she asked, trying for a casual, conversational tone.

'Not bad,' he responded without opening his eyes. 'This early in the season it's not too crowded.'

'It gets crowded up there?'

'You wouldn't believe it. I've known times when they've been sleeping two or three to a bunk in the huts, and more bivouacked outside. And in the summer the best ascents are swarming with bunches of students who barely know what they're doing, or even outright amateurs paying a guide to drag them up on the end of a rope.'

'Doesn't that make it rather dangerous?'

He opened one eye, and slanted her a glance of sardonic amusement. 'Climbing's always dangerous for fools,' he said. 'They don't even need to come to the Alps to get themselves killed—you can break your neck falling off the sea-cliffs at Brean Down.'

'But even experts sometimes have accidents,' she pointed out. 'Doesn't that worry you?'

'I try not to think about it,' he responded lazily. 'If you never took any risks just because you were afraid of the consequences, you'd lead a pretty dull life.'

She didn't answer that. He was right, of course, though she didn't like to admit it. She was one of those who rarely took risks; she liked to think of herself as sensible—it was only rarely that she allowed herself to consider the possibility that she might be missing something. 'So did you get to the top?' she asked him.

'We weren't aiming for the top, not this time, though I expect we would have decided to go right up Mont Blanc if the weather held. But there are dozens of smaller peaks, the best rock-faces you'll find anywhere, and the glaciers are still in good condition at this time of year. You can go out about four in the morning and climb for the best part of the day, coming down to the next hut just a few miles on from where you started out. Then the next day you move on again, trekking all over the mountains.'

'Oh—I see. It sounds like hard work,' she commented.

'It is—but it's fun too. To sit and watch the sunset after a long, strenuous day, with a cup of ice-cold water melted from the glacier in one hand and a thick wedge of French bread and cheese in the other—that's sheer heaven.'

As they had been talking, a stunning blonde on the next sun-lounger had apparently decided that she needed to rub on a little more sun-tan oil. She had sat up, posing effectively to show off the lush perfection of her naked breasts, and was rubbing the oil into her gleaming skin with slow, sensuous strokes. Her golden hair tumbled in a glossy mane around her shoulders, and her pink lips were pouted to show a glimpse of even white teeth. Matt would have been less than human if he could have avoided admiring the view.

The girl glanced around, as if aware of his presence for the first time—but if Matt was deceived Caroline certainly wasn't. 'Oh, excuse me,' she purred in a pure Southern Belle drawl. She held out the bottle of oil to Matt. 'Ah just can't reach mah back. Would you oblige?'

'Of course.' There was something predatory about his smile as he moved over to her. Caroline glared at them both in disgust—of all the blatant pick-ups! For all the girl knew, Matt could have been her husband—but little would she care, by the look of her.

She was giggling as he trickled the oil along her spine. 'Ooh—that tickles!' she protested, the beam of her blue eyes telling him she didn't mind at all.

He laughed, a low, intimate chuckle, as he

began to massage her gleaming skin. Caroline turned away from them and began to stuff her belongings quickly into her beach-bag. 'Well, if you'll excuse me,' she remarked caustically, 'I think I'll go and get some lunch.'

'OK—I'll see you later,' was all the response she got.

She stood up, and with as much dignity as she could muster stalked away across the beach.

Cannes was packed: the roads were choked with traffic, the pavements surged with crowds, eddying in excitement now and then as a big celebrity was spotted. The sea was incredibly blue beneath the high bright sun, the long golden strand of the beach, the bustling boulevard with its gleaming white hotels and beds of bright flowers beneath waving emerald-green palm trees—in the clear air the scene had the precise definition of a Hockney painting.

The whole festival fortnight was one long jamboree of galas and beach parties. Caroline hated it. But Matt would be in his element—all those luscious, half-naked beauties that decorated the beach every day, displaying their assets in the hope of catching the right eye, posing provocatively in the surf in the time-honoured way for the flocks of photographers.

What did fate have against her, arranging for him to bump into her mother like that? It was one more coincidence that she didn't need. It had been three weeks since the night of the Academy dinner, and she had been doing her best to avoid him—not easy within the close-knit legal fraternity of the Inns of Court, especially when they were in the same set of Chambers. But, to be honest, he had shown no signs of wishing to seek her out.

But now everything had been turned upside-down again. An odd little shimmer of heat ran through her as she remembered the way he had looked at her down on the beach. There had been something strangely intimate in his eyes—as if she had taken her clothes off just for him.

What would she do if he decided he wanted to take it further? Matthew Farrar-Reid had earned himself quite a reputation—not many women seemed able to resist his charm. She could only imagine what kind of sorcery he employed to get his way. It must be his eyes that did it. Sometimes he could look at you as if. . .

Damn, what was she doing, letting herself think like that? Maybe it had crossed his mind fleetingly to try to see how far he could go with her, but that blonde had very quickly distracted him. And very fortunate it was too. With an impatient shake of her head, Caroline dismissed him resolutely from her mind, and finding a gap in the traffic dodged across the road to her hotel.

Her parents had taken one of the best suites in the hotel, on the first floor, overlooking the wide sweep of La Croisette. It was quiet up here, the double glazing on the windows insulating it from the razzmatazz outside. Her footsteps didn't make a sound on the thick-piled apricot and blue carpet.

She padded into her own bedroom and stripped off her T-shirt and bikini briefs, and then strolled through into the exotic black-tiled bathroom to take a nice refreshing shower. The soft needles of water soothed away the tensions that had been aroused by Matt's unexpected arrival.

So what if he was staying at the hotel? He was unlikely to bother her. There were more than enough beautiful—and available—women in the town to keep him fully entertained. She stepped out of the shower and scrubbed herself vigorously dry on a large, fluffy towel.

The big mirror above the vanity unit showed her a reflection of her naked body, and she stood for a moment, studying herself critically. She wasn't bad-looking, even if she said so herself. The sun had tinted her skin to a warm honey-gold that looked good with her brown eyes and glossy, mahogany-coloured hair. And her cautious approach to sunbathing was paying off—her skin had none of the leathery look she had seen on some women, younger than herself, who spent too long in the sun.

Her figure was quite good too. Of course, she swam regularly, and took an aerobics dance class at the health centre near her Putney flat. Her legs were long and slim, her midriff slender, her breasts firm and shapely enough to warrant the approval that had registered in Matt's eyes. Dammit, she was letting herself think about those eyes again! She was going to have to be careful—that man was dangerous!

After lunch, she decided to go and sit on the terrace at the front of the hotel. She could have a cool drink, read one of the thick paperbacks she had brought with her, and watch the world go by. She had chosen to wear a plain white cotton dress, severely styled like a man's shirt, and she had put on her forbidding glasses—but contrarily she had left her hair loose down her back, brushing it until it gleamed like polished wood.

And some unconscious impulse had suggested that she draw in her tiny waist with a wide leather belt and leave the top two buttons of the dress tantalisingly unfastened. After all, even though no one was going to be taking any notice of her amid the galaxy of starlets gathered for the festival, there was no need for her to look dowdy.

In fact she received several flattering glances, though she kept all her attention focused on the devious doings of *Smiley's People*. Even when Matt appeared on the far side of the road, laughing with that blonde as they climbed the steps from the beach, she took no notice.

The pair of them crossed the road and came towards the hotel. Caroline kept her eyes resolutely on her page. He had seen her. He parted from the blonde as if they were old friends, and began threading his way between the white-clothed tables. The cane chair opposite her creaked as he sat down.

'Ah he said. 'The mystery is solved.'

She would have liked to be able to ignore him, but that would have been too obvious, so reluctantly she lowered her book. 'What mystery?'

'I was beginning to think there were two of you,' he explained with a provocative smile. 'Caroline Kosek, strait-laced barrister-at-law, and the stunning creature in the flamingo dress. But now the two images have merged. Though I must confess,' he added provocatively, 'I prefer what you were wearing earlier.'

Her eyes flashed him a frosty warning, and she picked up her drink, the ice clinking against the glass as her hand shook.

'I hope you're not hitting the brandy again,' he remarked.

'Perrier water,' she retorted crisply. 'Not that it's any of your business.'

'Just a little friendly concern.'

'I don't recall that we were ever friends,' she snapped, and instantly bit her tongue.

He laughed softly. 'Now, what on earth have I done to deserve that?' he taunted.

Caroline drew in a slow breath, struggling for some semblance of composure. The last thing she wanted was to let him think he was having some effect on her. 'I wasn't particularly keen on being stared at this morning as if I were this month's centrefold,' she responded with dignity.

He smiled slowly. 'I'm sorry,' he said, his voice taking on a husky timbre. 'But it did come as something of a surprise—whoever would have thought that the prudish Miss Kosek was hiding such a delicious body under her drab courtroom black?'

Her eyes flew to his face. 'I am not prudish!' she protested, stung.

'No?' The way he was looking at her made her heart skid and start to race at twice its normal speed. 'Hmm—now that's a very interesting revelation.'

Before she could catch her breath, her parents appeared on the terrace, and her mother waved as she dragged her father over to them. 'Ah, there you are, you two,' she greeted them archly. 'I hope we aren't interrupting anything. Adam, you remember Caroline's young man, don't you? Matthew's come down to join us for a couple of weeks.'

'Of course,' beamed Adam, the exact circumstances of their previous meeting apparently quite forgotten.

As Matt rose to shake her father's hand, Caroline tried to catch her mother's eye to warn her to guard her tactless tongue, but it was a waste of time. 'Now you *will* be coming with us tonight, won't you, Matthew?' she ran on blithely. 'It's a Czechoslovakian film—I always think they're so *meaningful*, don't you? And of course, Adam is one of the judges.'

'Thank you,' Matt responded gravely. 'I would be delighted to come—unfortunately, however, I don't have the proper clothes with me.'

'Oh, that's no problem!' her mother assured him quickly. 'Adam will lend you something, won't you, dear? I'm sure you must be about the same size. Good heavens, we can't leave you stuck here in the hotel all by yourself!'

Caroline suppressed a dry smile. She was quite sure that Matt would be more than adequately entertained. He slanted her a glance of mocking amusement, and turned back to her mother. 'Then I'd be delighted to come. I hope it won't be any inconvenience, sir?'

'Of course not,' Adam assured him graciously. 'Come on upstairs and we'll see what we can find.'

The two men went off together, and Betty sat

down. 'He likes him,' she confided to Caroline, as if it were news of world-shattering importance.

'Mother,' began Caroline patiently, 'could we just get one thing absolutely clear? Matthew Farrar-Reid is *not* my "young man"—we merely work together, and it was no more than coincidence that he happened to be in Cannes.'

Betty blinked at her in dumb surprise, then smiled understandingly. 'Yes, dear—of course,' she agreed conspiratorially. Caroline sighed. Her mother had watched too many of her father's slushy romantic films.

She would have worn the green dress anyway. It really was rather beautiful—the colour was a rich jade, the fabric shimmering silk that draped elegantly into a neat bow over one hip and flowed in a smooth line to the floor. It had a hint of the thirties about it, and something about the way it moved made her want to waltz.

She twisted her hair up into a thick, gleaming coil, and clasped a fine gold chain around her throat. Surveying her reflection in the mirror, she had to admit she was quite pleased. The glowing colour suited the warm tones of her skin and hair, and the stylish cut flattered her graceful figure.

Matt had arrived—she could hear the sound of his voice in the next room, talking to her father. For a moment she hesitated, trying to control the nervous excitement in her stomach. Of course, it wasn't like going out with him in the ordinary way—her parents would be there, for one thing. And besides, he had only come out of politeness to her mother—he would probably prefer to be with that dumb blonde.

Well, she was just going to look on it as yet another dull evening watching a boring film. That was something she had done often enough—and often with an escort who wanted to be with her as little as she wanted to be with him. Taking a deep, steadying breath and holding her head up with pride, she opened the door.

He had made himself comfortable in one of the big, squashy hide-upholstered sofas, and he glanced up as she came into the room. A slow smile of approval curved his arrogant mouth, and he rose to his feet, his manner irreproachably polite, though the gleam in his blue eyes made her heart flutter alarmingly.

'Well,' he murmured. 'You look absolutely stunning.'

Caroline acknowledged his flattery with a slight inclination of her head as she sat down. 'Thank you,' she responded coolly.

'Yes, not bad at all,' her father agreed readily. 'I dare say we'll have to wait for your mother,' he added with weary patience. 'That woman has no concept of time.'

'Now, now,' his wife chided him, bustling into the room. 'I wouldn't dream of being late for something as important as this!'

'Ah, good, so you're ready. Well, let's get going, then—we don't want to keep the car waiting.'

But, in spite of his words, he seemed to be in no particular hurry; he always liked to be one of the last to arrive—he felt it made a bigger impact. However, at last they really did set off. A white

Rolls-Royce was waiting to pick them up outside the hotel, though it was barely a quarter of a mile to the Palais des Festivals.

But the car was essential to get them through the crowds that were gathered outside. The Palais rose above the Old Port, a layered white building, lit up like some great ocean liner. As the car drew up before the imposing entrance the crowd surged forward, fans and photographers, all eager for one of Adam Kosek's famous smiles.

Matt didn't seem to be the least bit disconcerted by all the fuss. He helped Caroline from the car, and she let her hand rest lightly on his arm as they followed her parents into the narrow channel the security people had cleaved through the crowds. Maybe he would think that the nervous tremor that had run through her body as she had touched him was due to the crush.

A glittering champagne reception waited for them before the start of the film. But the first person Caroline saw across the room was the blonde from the beach. She was wearing a slinky black dress that seemed to stay up in defiance of all the laws of gravity and moulded her curvaceous figure like a glove, and her hair shone like gold, catching every light.

She was with a white-haired man whom Caroline recognised as one of the casting-couch school of film producers, but as soon as she saw Matt she flashed him a wide smile, and a moment later she was dragging her bemused companion across the room towards them.

'Hi, Matt,' she murmured breathily. 'Ah didn't know you were coming here tonight.'

Any man less self-assured than Matthew Farrar-Reid might have been embarrassed, but he handled the situation with all his usual sang-froid. 'Hello, Anthea. Caroline, I don't believe you two have met.'

The girl cast her one assessing glance, and dismissed the competition, turning back to Matt. 'Ah've been telling Honey-Bear all about you,' she confided to Matt. Caroline winced at the awful pet name. 'He said he couldn't wait to meet you, didn't you, Sugar-Plum? Don't you think it would be just fabulous to make a film about mountain-climbing? It's so exciting!'

'I hardly think it would make much of a film,' Matt demurred drily.

'Oh, but it *would*! What about that story you were telling me this afternoon? About when you climbed the. . .the Arnold something. . .'

'The Aven Armand,' he corrected her, smiling. 'And it's a cave, not a mountain.'

'Oh.' She looked blank. 'Ah thought you climbed mountains?'

'I do both.'

She giggled cutely, batting her furry lashes. 'Well, Ah suppose there's not much difference— just that one goes down and the other goes up!'

The two men laughed tolerantly at her ignorance, but Caroline caught a glint of sharp calculation in those china-blue eyes. So Anthea wasn't as dumb as she was pretending to be—it was all an act, playing the kewpie doll to pander to the male ego. But, even if Honey-Bear was fooled, surely Matt could see through it?

She was glad when the announcement that the

judges were being invited to take their places brought the conversation to an end. With a polite word of farewell to Goldilocks and Honey-Bear, Matt led her up the stairs.

Her parents were in the front row, but she and Matt were half a dozen rows back. The plush seats were so comfortable that she was afraid she might fall asleep, especially as the film promised to be extremely boring—it had subtitles, and she didn't have her glasses.

'You know, it seemed to me that you didn't quite take to Anthea,' Matt murmured quietly as the opening credits rolled.

She turned him a wide-eyed, ingenuous look. 'Whatever gave you that impression?'

He laughed softly. 'Butter wouldn't melt in your mouth, would it?' he taunted.

Suddenly an alarming flutter had started in the pit of her stomach. He was so close, and beneath that urbane exterior there lurked a powerful, predatory male. Some primeval core of pure femininity inside her seemed to respond instinctively. Was that how his spell worked? Cautiously she eased her position, discreetly trying to edge away from him.

'I wonder, though,' he went on musingly. 'Sometimes still waters run deep. What lies behind that cool little smile of yours? It might be very interesting to find out.'

Her breath was warm on her lips. 'No, thank you,' she managed to say. 'If you're looking for entertainment, I've no doubt you'd find Anthea, or whatever her name is, more than willing to oblige.' The mocking curve of his mouth goaded her into adding tartly, 'If you can stand that nauseating giggle, of course.'

'Catty,' he derided with a shade of triumph. 'I might almost think you were a little jealous.'

'Huh!'

One or two people around them had turned towards her, and she realised that she had spoken a little too loudly. She subsided into an angry silence, glad of the darkness in the auditorium to hide the flame in her cheeks.

CHAPTER FOUR

THE film was every bit as dull as Caroline had expected, and she let her eyes wander instead around the small theatre. Anthea and her Honey-Bear were two rows in front of them. Caroline studied the girl covertly in the darkness. She was certainly beautiful. But surely Matt couldn't really be attracted by that sugary feminine act?

She smiled wryly to herself. It wasn't her personality he was interested in—like any red-blooded male, he would be hungry to get his hands on that gorgeous body that was displayed so provocatively. But what game was Anthea playing? Surely she wouldn't risk angering her film producer for the sake of a quick fling with another man, however attractive? Or maybe she just had some compulsive urge to collect every scalp she could.

Anyway, why should she care? It wasn't as if she wanted him for herself. . .Suddenly her pulse began to race as her thoughts conjured up the most vivid images. What would it be like to be held in those strong arms, to feel the brush of those firm, warm lips on hers, to surrender to his expert caresses?

Bewildered, she fought to suppress the tide of sensuous longing that threatened to sweep away her sanity. What was happening to her? Were the sun, the sea air, the decadent, anything-goes attitudes all around her, undermining her reason?

The last thing she wanted was to succumb to a man like that. She had seen too much of the cynical way her father used women to gratify his own ego ever to want to risk getting caught by the same tricks. But, thrown together like this, away from the strictly observed etiquette that ruled their working life. . .If he chose to turn that fatal charm on her . . .

Impatiently she pushed that thought from her mind. After all, she wasn't some dumb bimbo, at the mercy of her hormones. She was an intelligent woman, accustomed to exercising self-control. *If* Matt Farrar-Reid decided to amuse himself at her expense, she would just. . .put him firmly in his place.

At long, long last the film came to an end. There was a ripple of polite applause, and everyone immediately began to fidget. 'Thank heavens that's over,' sighed Caroline wearily.

Matt slanted her a teasing smile. 'You didn't like it?'

'Did you?'

'I admired the director's use of eclectic symbolism to convey a forceful sense of narrative. . .'

Caroline gurgled with laughter.

'I said something funny?' he enquired, only the depths of his eyes betraying his amusement.

'I'm quite sure everyone else will be saying much the same thing,' she responded drily. 'Come on, let's go and grab some more champagne before it's all gone.'

She had been right in her assessment. Down in

the foyer, many of those who had been overtly yawning—indeed some who had quite definitely been asleep—were now eager to discuss the director's radically introspective standpoint or the stylish devices used in the climactic scene.

'Let's get out of here,' suggested Matt, taking her arm.

She was more than ready to agree. But as they reached the main doors, whether by accident or design, Anthea arrived there too, still with Honey-Bear in tow.

'Matt! Are you going on?' she cried eagerly. 'We're going to try that new nightclub on the Rue Macé. It's *the* place. Do come!'

He glanced down at Caroline, a question in his eyes. She felt a surge of angry disappointment—for a foolish moment she had thought he wanted to be with *her*. 'Don't let me stop you,' she enunciated in glacial accents.

'You don't want to come?'

'I'm afraid that sort of place isn't really my scene.'

'How do you know that without trying it?' he asked with maddening logic.

'I. . .' She couldn't think of a suitable retort. 'I just want to go back to the hotel,' she insisted with dignity.

He shrugged his wide shoulders in cool indifference. 'Suit yourself,' he conceded lazily. 'I'll see you later,' he added to Anthea, slanting her a smile that was ripe with meaning.

Caroline stiffened, drawing away from him. 'I can find my own way home, thank you,' she informed him.

'I brought you, I'll take you home,' he responded firmly.

'I *came* with my parents. . .'

'Who are going off somewhere else, by the look of it,' he pointed out, glancing towards where Betty and Adam were making ready to leave with a party of their own generation, not even noticing their daughter.

Caroline took a deep breath, counting slowly to ten as she fought to subdue the turmoil of her emotions. 'Very well,' she conceded tightly. 'Thank you.'

They walked in frigid silence along the boulevard. It was still quite busy, but even so the romantic beauty of the evening inveigled her senses. The sky was a deep violet blue, spangled with a million stars that reflected like diamonds in the whispering sea, and the warm night air was fragrant with the essence of pine and orange-blossom and wild herbs that blended a perfume that was pure Côte d'Azur.

She risked a covert glance towards her companion. He was strolling along with that long, lazy stride, the elegant white dinner jacket casually thrown open and his hands deep in the pockets of his black trousers.

She was becoming increasingly confused by what was happening between them. Sometimes Matt really seemed to be attracted to her, seemed almost to be flirting with her—then at other times such a notion seemed quite ridiculous. She must be imagining it all—and yet she had never believed that she was a vain person.

It had been all too plain that this insistence on

escorting her home had been dictated only by good manners, and that he intended to join Anthea at her nightclub as soon as possible. Yet moments earlier they had been sharing the discovery of a similar sense of humour—it had seemed that they had been on exactly the same wavelength.

And as they crossed the road towards their hotel she began to wonder how far he would escort her—to the foyer, to the lift. . .to the door of the suite? An odd little twist of tension began to coil inside her. It increased as she collected her key, increased further as they rode up in the lift. It wasn't necessary for him to come this far, unless. . .unless he planned to try to kiss her goodnight.

Her hand was shaking as she tried to fit the key into the lock. She felt him move very close behind her, and some reflex of defence made her defer the problem by blurting out, 'Would you like a drink?' As soon as she had said it, she realised that she had only made things worse by inviting him into the suite, so she added stiffly, 'Before you go on to wherever you're going.'

'Thank you.'

She couldn't quite interpret his smile. She preceded him into the room, her spine very erect. 'What would you like?' she managed to ask.

'I'll have a brandy, if you've got any.'

'Yes, of course.' She tossed her handbag into an armchair and crossed the room to the well-stocked bar. 'Ice?'

'Yes, please.'

He had followed her, and again her hand was

shaking as she unstopped the decanter and sloshed a generous measure into the glass. As she turned to hand it to him, she found that he was very close indeed. Her breath stopped in her throat as she stared up into those hypnotic blue eyes.

'You know, I like your hair like that,' he murmured softly. 'But I like it even better loose.'

Caroline stood transfixed as he deftly found the pins that held the heavy coil in place and drew them out to let the rich mahogany tresses tumble around her shoulders. 'There,' he approved, letting one long silken strand trail through his fingers. 'The transformation is really quite incredible. Suddenly the austere Miss Kosek is an altogether more enticing creature.'

Very slowly he wound a thick hank of hair around his hand, imprisoning her. As he drew her close, and his head bent over hers, her lips parted instinctively. He paused, smiling as if he hadn't expected such an easy victory, and a wave of humiliation flooded through her.

But, as he took the tumbler of brandy from her numb fingers and drew her into his arms, she didn't know how to resist. Suddenly she had an overpowering need to know what it would be like to be kissed by him. Her only defence was to close her eyes, unable to meet the molten heat in his.

His mouth brushed her trembling eyelids with a feather-light touch, found a fluttering pulse beneath her temple, warmed the delicate shell of her ear. She felt the hot tip of his tongue teasing the sensitive spot at the corner of her lips, and she moaned softly, turning her head hungrily to seek his kiss.

He laughed, low in his throat, and drew her
hard against him, his hand sliding slowly down
her back to mould intimately over the base of her
spine. His teeth nipped sensuously into the vulnerable softness of her lower lip, and blindly she
reached up to wrap her arms around his neck,
curving her supple body into his demanding
embrace, unconscious of the vivid messages she
was conveying, conscious only of her own urgent
need.

She had never been kissed like this before. Years
ago, at university, she had succumbed to curiosity
a few times, allowed some kisses and even a little
petting, just to find out what all the fuss was
about. She hadn't been impressed.

But this was totally different. As Matt's tongue
plundered deep into the secret corners of her
mouth, she could only surrender. His caressing
hand moved slowly over her body, burning her
soft flesh through the silky fabric of her dress. A
delicious tension was building inside her, and as
his palm brushed over the ripe swell of her breast
she breathed a ragged sigh of pure pleasure. His
thumb was teasing the hardened, sensitised bud
of her nipple, sending a million exquisite sensa-
tions through her taut nerve-fibres.

But then, through the darkness swirling in her
brain, she heard his soft, mocking laughter. 'Well,
it seems I was guilty of libel,' he murmured
huskily. 'You're certainly no prude!'

Caroline froze in shock, reality flooding back in
a chill tide. 'Let me go! How dare you?' she
gasped, pushing him away. 'Get out of here this
minute or I'll . . . I'll call the manager!'

He lifted a sardonic eyebrow, infuriatingly cool. 'You invited me in for a drink,' he reminded her.

'Well, now I want you to leave,' she insisted tensely. Her shame at the wanton way she had behaved made her retreat into defensive anger. She marched over and jerked the door open. 'Anthea will be waiting for you,' she added in a voice that dripped sarcasm.

He smiled knowingly. 'What makes you think that I'm interested in Anthea?'

'Oh, nothing,' she bit at him. 'Only the way you were looking at her as if she was your next meal.'

'Ah! Well, yes, I agree she's a succulent morsel—but there would be little there to really satisfy a man's appetites. Whereas you—you're much more of a challenge.' His voice had taken on a huskier timbre, and his eyes slid over her with an insolent intimacy that made her cheeks flame scarlet. 'And I never could resist a challenge. The tougher the climb, the icier and more treacherous the mountain, the greater the satisfaction when you're standing right there on top.'

His words sent an odd little shiver through her as she recognised the force of that predatory male desire for dominance, for mastery. And, to her horror, some irrational part of her mind ached to respond. But fortunately a few shreds of sanity remained, and she forced herself to meet that mocking gaze unflinchingly.

'Please go now,' she repeated in a voice that came from outer space.

He laughed softly, provocatively. 'Very well,' he conceded. 'But you know, we've got nearly two more weeks here. Shall we make a little bet on the outcome of this game? I'm confident that before we leave, I'll have you in my bed.' He picked up his forgotten tumbler of brandy and downed it in one draught. 'Goodnight, Miss Kosek.'

She closed the door behind him, and sank weakly into an armchair. She was shaking, tears of humiliation stinging the backs of her eyes. She was all too afraid that he was right—if he deliberately set out to seduce her, she didn't have any weapons to fight him. And if she succumbed, if she let him make love to her, how on earth was she going to face him when they got back to London?

Caroline slept badly, and was not in the best of moods when she went down to the sunny terrace in front of the hotel next morning to join her mother for a late breakfast. She might have guessed that Matt would already be there, sharing her mother's table. She hesitated, but at that moment Betty looked up, and waved.

'Ah, here you are at last,' she greeted her. 'I've just been scolding Matthew,' she added archly. 'I thought he must have kept you up dreadfully late last night.'

'Not at all,' responded Caroline coolly as she took her seat. 'I came straight home after the screening.'

'Oh.' Betty looked a little taken aback, but she quickly recovered with, 'Now then, what are you two young people going to do today? Do you water-ski, Matthew? Caroline does—she's very good. And this evening we've all been invited to sail down to Monte and lose lots of lovely money in the casino. You will come, won't you?'

'I'd love to,' he agreed readily, ignoring the fulminating light in Caroline's eyes. 'I don't usually gamble, but maybe tonight I'll be lucky.'

Caroline's palm itched to slap that arrogant face, but Betty was beaming with satisfaction, innocently unaware of the dark undercurrents of tension.

'Good, that's settled. Now, you must excuse me—I've promised to go into Nice with a couple of the girls. Have a lovely day, the two of you.'

Matt rose politely to his feet as Betty fussed with her bag and her sun-glasses and bent to peck Caroline on the cheek. As he sat down again, Caroline studied him covertly from beneath her lashes. What had he done after he had left her last night?

She didn't want to ask, but she just couldn't help herself. 'So, how was the fabulous new night-club?' she enquired stiffly. 'Did you enjoy yourself?'

'Yes, thank you,' he responded, a glint of sardonic amusement in his eyes. 'You should have come.'

'It isn't the sort of thing I enjoy.'

He laughed softly. 'So, today we're back to the strait-laced Miss Kosek, are we?' he taunted. 'What's happened to the eminently desirable Caroline? Have you put her back in her box?'

'I'm afraid she's entirely a product of your imagination,' she countered repressively.

'Oh, I don't deal in imagination,' he murmured provocatively. 'I deal in facts. Point one, Your

Honour, the lady looked at me with those big, beautiful brown eyes, and how could a red-blooded male resist such an invitation? Point two, she didn't try to push me away. In fact she responded so willingly, it was a wonder I didn't ravish her on the spot. Point three . . .'

'Very funny. Save your witty remarks for the luscious Anthea,' she advised caustically. 'Though I doubt if she'll understand half of them.'

'Jealous?'

She studiously ignored him as she reached for a croissant.

'Your father was at the club last night, by the way,' he went on.

Her head jerked up. 'Dad? But. . .He was with my mother. They went off with the other judges,' she protested.

'I don't know where your mother was. He arrived pretty late—it was getting on for three. He didn't stay long.'

'Who was he with?' she asked with difficulty.

'There was a group of them—half a dozen. I couldn't see if he was with anyone special.'

Caroline sighed with resignation. 'If there was a blonde, that was who he was with,' she surmised from long experience. She might have known it was too good to be true, the calm that had reigned between her parents for the past few weeks since the night of the Academy dinner.

Those shrewd blue eyes were studying her face. 'I suppose it isn't really surprising that you're scared of men, if that's the sort of example you've grown up with,' he mused far too perceptively.

'I'm not scared of men,' she protested, her voice

choking. Her eyes refused to meet his. 'I just. . .prefer to concentrate on my career.'

'You know, you're missing out on one of the sweetest pleasures in life.'

'Oh? You mean going to bed with you?' she retorted with biting sarcasm.

Matt shook his head, laughing. 'My ego's not quite that big! But you obviously know what I mean. The way you responded last night when I kissed you. . .'

Caroline felt a slow blush rise over her cheeks. The memory of that kiss was so vivid, she could still feel the heat of his lips on hers, feel the touch of his hand caressing her body. 'I . . . I don't think sex is all it's cracked up to be,' she retorted defensively.

'Don't you?' She went rigid with shock as his hand covered hers, and his thumb began to circle sensuously over the inside of her wrist. 'Maybe you've been unfortunate in your choice of lovers.'

She jerked her hand away so sharply that she sent a plate crashing to the floor. She bent over to pick up the shattered pieces, aware that her action had drawn every eye to them. She was furious with embarrassment. But as she straightened, ready to bite his head off, an all-too-familiar Texan drawl hailed him from across the terrace.

'Matt! Hi, are you coming down to the beach?' Anthea was looking sensational in tiny white shorts and a sugar-pink T-shirt that clung to every contour.

Matt lifted his hand in greeting. 'I'll be right with you. What are you doing today?' he added to Caroline.

'I have some shopping to do,' she responded stiffly.

He smiled that slow, knowing smile that made her feel so transparent. 'What a pity. But still, we'll meet again tonight, and we can both try our luck—at the casino.'

She felt a flush of pink steal over her cheeks at his deliberate invocation of his challenge of last night. The look in his eyes underlined the message, and she turned her head away quickly, to let her eyes be dazzled by the sparkling reflection of the sun on the sea.

She had no intention of watching him go, but she couldn't help seeing the familiar way he dropped his arm around the blonde girl's shoulders, or the way they were laughing together as they strolled across the road. Her fist clenched into a tight ball. Matt was an expert at this game, of which she knew nothing. But she couldn't let him win—because, to her, it wouldn't be a game.

She might have known that Anthea would be among the guests aboard the luxurious yacht that evening. The shorts and T-shirt she was wearing were even skimpier than those she had had on that morning, and were drawing a considerable amount of male attention her way. Caroline slanted her a glance of cold disdain—she must be really desperate to be the centre of attention, to flaunt herself in that way.

Suddenly she caught herself up with a thud of shock. She *was* jealous—she had no other reason to feel quite such a burning dislike for the girl. And that was Matt's fault—he was deliberately playing the situation to his own advantage. She hated him for that.

'Betty, Adam! Lovely to see you, darlings!' Their host swept forward to welcome them aboard, liberal with hugs and kisses.

Her mother responded effusively. 'Darling! You remember my daughter Caroline? And this is her young man.'

Matt accepted the sobriquet with a smile of faintly sardonic humour. And yet Caroline was aware of a certain pride in being at his side. Everyone was casually dressed for the outward cruise, and he was wearing a pair of pale blue trousers and a crisp white cotton shirt—the cuffs were folded back over his strong brown wrists, and the collar was open, revealing an interesting glimpse of rough, sun-bleached hair curling at the base of his throat.

He too was drawing a considerable amount of attention, and it wasn't only the women who were aware of his presence. Several of the vain young actors plainly objected to this amateur competition. They, who had built their muscles in expensive gymnasiums and had their hair fashionably sun-streaked in the most stylish salons, knew the real thing when they saw it.

She had told herself that she could cope, that she could keep him at arm's length, but now that she was with him again she was all too aware of how vulnerable she was. She would find herself watching him, remembering the way those strong arms had held her; sometimes when she was close to him she would breathe a hint of that evocative male muskiness of his body, and the images that stirred in her brain would heat her blood to a fever.

It was a beautiful evening to be sailing along the lovely coastline of the Côte d'Azur. The sea was calm, sparkling in the sun, and the rocky, pine-clad hills and tiny villages were like picture-post-card scenes. They sailed slowly across the wide sweep of the Baie des Anges and around Cap Ferrat, and docked in the yacht harbour at Monte Carlo as the sun began to set. The towering apart-ment blocks that ringed the bay were coming alight, while behind them the encircling hills were fading into the evening sky.

The guests all adjourned to change into their evening finery. Down in one of the sumptuous state-rooms, the air was thick with barbed compli-ments as a dozen women shared the cramped accommodation. Caroline was doing her best to ignore Anthea—not easy, as her voice carried above everybody else's.

'. . .getting a bit too much—you know what Ah mean. He thinks he *owns* me. To be honest, Ah won't mind if his wife *does* show up.'

I just bet you won't, Caroline thought tartly. It'll leave you free to chase after Matt. She paused in the act of putting up her hair. Maybe she'd wear it loose tonight for a change. The dress she had chosen was quite plain—a cinnamon-coloured silk, shot through with the faintest shimmer of gold. Anthea, on the other hand, was in silver lurex, slashed to the waist—far too obvious for Matt's taste, surely?

A startled expression sprang to her eyes. Had she been reduced to *competing* with a girl like

Anthea? The thought was humiliating. She hesitated. It was too late to change her hair—the
others were already making their way upstairs.
Quickly she snatched up her glasses and slid them
on to her nose—at least with them on it wouldn't
look as if she had been trying to dress to please
him.

Their party swept through Monte Carlo like a
blazing meteor. Even in that dazzling square mile,
knee-deep in billionaires, such a cast of unrestrained extroverts could turn heads—especially as
the gallons of champagne that had been consumed
on the yacht and in the restaurant where they
dined began to take effect.

Caroline had been to the casino before, several
times, but she never ceased to be fascinated by the
atmosphere—she loved the voluptuous caryatids
in the ornate foyer and the cigar-smoking nymphs
on the frescoed ceiling in the Salon Rose.

'Aren't you playing tonight?' her mother asked.

She shook her head. 'No—I'll watch you.'

'I feel lucky tonight,' Betty confided, her eyes
alight with excitement. 'I've got my lucky earrings
on.' She laughed flirtatiously at Matt. 'I have my
very own system. You'll think it's silly. I always
use our birthdays.' Matt smiled politely. 'Perhaps
I should include yours,' she dimpled. 'What is it?'

'August the fourteenth.'

'Oh! Then you're a Leo. I guessed you must be!
And fourteen—yes, that sounds like a lucky
number. Let me see now, where is it?' She peered
across the green baize, and set down a pile of
chips.

Caroline smiled ruefully—her mother was an

infrequent but very enthusiastic gambler, and would probably sit over the table for hours. She glanced around for her father. He was on the far side of the room—standing very close to a doe-eyed blonde of his favourite type. Well, at least her mother was likely to be too absorbed in the play to notice.

Anthea was at the same table as Betty, gambling wildly with Honey-Bear's chips and giggling like a little girl every time she lost. 'Oh, dear,' she pouted cutely as the croupier raked away yet another pile of chips, 'Ah'm afraid Ah'm just no good at figures.' She let her body sway provocatively as she spoke, inviting the obvious compliment, which Honey-Bear obligingly supplied.

Caroline couldn't quite suppress a pained sigh, and Matt lifted a sardonic eyebrow. 'You're not amused?'

She returned him a chilly glance. 'She isn't exactly. . .my type of person,' she responded stiffly.

'No, I suppose not,' he mused. He watched as Anthea staked another pile of chips, a small smile on his arrogant mouth as she slanted him a flirtatious glance across the table, batting her unreal eyelashes and dipping forward to emphasise those lush curves. 'She certainly knows how to enjoy herself, though.'

And I don't? Stupidly, that hurt. Was that how he saw her—dull, strait-laced. . .*boring*? She lapsed into a pensive silence. Suddenly it seemed as though she was seeing her whole life from a different perspective—and she didn't much like what she saw. The past and the future passed before her eyes, arid and empty. . .lonely.

For the rest of the evening she felt as if she were watching the fun through a pane of glass, unable to make contact. It was quite a relief when at last some of the party began to suggest calling it a night and heading back to the yacht.

In fact it was almost dawn as they strolled down the steep hill towards the harbour. The normally busy streets were almost deserted—a road-sweeping cart laboured noisily up the hill, and a little Fiat pick-up laden with crates of fresh fruit came down the other way. The sky had faded to mother-of-pearl, and the sea sparkled pale gold, telling them the sun had risen above the horizon, although they couldn't yet see it, down in the harbour at the bottom of the great bowl of the surrounding hills.

The straggling party staggered aboard the yacht, some of them making straight for the cabins to collapse on the beds, others to sit around in the luxurious saloon making desultory conversation and trying a little hair-of-the-dog to ward off their incipient hangovers.

Caroline strolled out on deck to watch the sun climb the sky, rolling back the mist from the hills. The breeze tangled her hair, and she brushed it back impatiently from her face. Suddenly a shadow fell across the deck beside her, making her heart skip with alarm.

Matt had discarded his jacket and tie and rolled back his shirt-cuffs. She pretended to ignore his presence, continuing to gaze out over the sparkling water as the coastline slid by. But a tension of apprehension was knotting in her stomach. Why had he followed her? They were all alone out here. . .

CHAPTER FIVE

'THIS is my favourite time of day,' he mused, leaning his hands on the rail beside her. 'So fresh and clean—especially after a night like that.'

'You spend many nights like that?' Caroline enquired, her voice infused with lukewarm disdain.

He laughed drily. 'Not as many as rumour claims.'

She stiffened as he moved towards her, but when he put up his hand it was only to tilt her glasses. 'Why are you wearing these?' he enquired, a lilt of mocking amusement in his voice.

'So that I can see,' she responded tautly.

He laughed softly. 'You wear them as if they're some sort of defence against the world,' he commented with unnerving perception. 'What are you so afraid of?'

'N. . .nothing,' she stammered, backing away from him.

'Then why don't you take them off?' He was moving towards her, until she found herself backed up against one of the for'ard bulkheads. 'They're going to get in the way.'

She stared up at him, her heart pounding. 'In the way of what?' she whispered.

'In the way of this.'

He lifted the offending glasses off her nose, and his head bent swiftly over hers, capturing her lips as they parted on a small gasp of shock. For an instant she tried to resist, but as she felt the languorous swirl of his tongue over the sensitive inner membranes of her mouth, kindling a melting heat inside her, all rational thought evaporated from her brain.

His kiss was pure temptation; what did it matter what happened when they got back to London? London was on another planet. All that mattered was this endless moment, and she surrendered herself totally to the pleasure of it. His body was crushing hers against the bulkhead, every inch pressed so intimately close that she could feel the warning tension of male arousal in him.

He wanted her—he really wanted *her*! There was no mistaking the urgency of his desire, and some deep, feminine instinct ached to meet that need. But it was all just a dream—a dream that could only end in pain and humiliation. Somehow she found the strength of will to push him away, and stood staring up at him, stunned by the effect that just one kiss could have.

'I. . .I. . .' She stepped back blindly, seeking to escape from him—and collided with the rail that ran around the deck. She felt herself overbalancing, and below her the white bow-wave foamed dizzylingly.

Matt caught her swiftly, laughing as he set her safely on her feet again. 'Now, come on,' he teased gently. 'There's no need to throw yourself overboard, just because I kissed you!'

Her agitation flamed into defensive fury. 'You arrogant pig!' she spat at him. 'You think you only have to snap your fingers, and every woman in

sight is going to fall at your feet. Well, not me.
Even if I *were* attracted to you—which I'm not!'

'No?' He laughed softly, shaking his head. 'Your
plea doesn't fit the evidence. If I were your counsel, I'd advise you to settle out of court.'

She felt her cheeks flame scarlet, and with an
angry flounce she turned away from him to stalk
back along the deck towards the main state-room.

'Er. . .Caro,' he called after her softly, 'haven't
you forgotten something?'

She paused, and slanted him an icy glance over
her shoulder. He was leaning against the for'ard
bulkhead, twirling her glasses casually between
his fingers. She hesitated reluctantly, and held out
her hand. 'Th. . .thank you,' she stammered.

His blue eyes glinted provocatively, daring her
to come closer. It was all she could do not to
snatch, and she pushed them quickly back on to
her nose, glaring at him angrily.

He studied her face with interest. 'Do you know,
maybe I was wrong about those glasses,' he
remarked. 'I think I rather like them. They make
you look. . .vulnerable.'

She made the mistake of looking up into his
eyes. The steel-blue had turned molten, mesmer-
ising her, and as he reached out his hand and
touched her cheek she swayed unconsciously
towards him. He let his finger coil into one long
strand of hair.

'What I don't understand,' he murmured, 'is
why you're so intent on trying to disguise the fact
that you're a very beautiful woman.' He drew her,
unresisting, into his arms. 'Why don't you just

relax, trust your instincts? All the time you refuse to take a chance, you're only half alive.'

She stared up at him, unable to think of a reply. His words were weaving a spell around her, undermining her will. She leaned her cheek against his hard chest, hearing the sound of his heartbeat, deep and strong—her own was racing. He was right—she *was* only half alive, except when she was in his arms. She closed her eyes, wishing the short hop along the Riviera coast were a long, slow voyage to China.

But it was barely thirty miles from Monte Carlo to Cannes, and as they passed between Ile Ste Marguerite and the Pointe, Caroline drew back, reluctant to let the dream end, but embarrassed by the way she had let herself give in to her own silly fantasies.

'Er. . .excuse me,' she mumbled, feeling extremely foolish. 'I. . .I'd better go and change before. . .before we dock.'

She made her escape before Matt could debate the matter, and hurried down to the cabin where she had left her day clothes. Her emotions were in turmoil—she was behaving just like the sort of silly, illogical female she despised in her father's films, falling for the fatal illusion of love.

Love—there was simply no logical basis to support its existence. It was an invention of poets and film producers, a conditioned response—a chemical reaction within the brain that triggered a flow of adrenalin, making the heart beat faster.

There was absolutely nothing unique or special about Matthew Farrar-Reid. Very well, so his features happened to have been arranged a little more attractively than most, so he had learned to smile in that certain way. That was the luck of genetic endowment, there was no magic about it.

Oh, but there was, her heart cried out. You couldn't subject love to logical argument. It just. . .*was*. As a perfect rose was more than just a fortuitous arrangement of perfume and petals. She sat down weakly on the edge of one of the beds. She had fallen in love with him.

It didn't make any kind of sense—in fact, it was just about the stupidest thing she could ever have done. She had told herself the first time she had met him that he was the sort of man that no woman of intelligence would ever consider getting herself tangled up with. But somehow she had— and there wasn't a damn thing she could do about it.

Except that she didn't have to let things get out of control, her head insisted firmly. That was what she had really always disliked about those mushy, sentimental films—the way the characters gave in to their emotions, and never mind the conse- quences. Well, she wasn't like that—she had a little self-discipline.

She couldn't avoid seeing Matt, but she could avoid being alone with him. And she could go on behaving in her usual cool, matter-of-fact way. That way, at least he would never guess—and maybe, in time, she would be able to convince her own heart that it wasn't true. In that resolute spirit, she grabbed her clothes quickly and began to change out of her evening-dress.

It was still early morning when the yacht nudged into its berth at the Port Pierre-Canto, but there was a car waiting there, and a slightly older version of Anthea stood beside it, impatience radiating from her in waves. And she wasn't calling her husband Honey-Bear either.

Her sharply raised voice could be heard clearly in the fresh morning air. 'Don't tell me you didn't get my telegram—I've heard that excuse a dozen times. I was expecting you to be at the airport to meet me. So where were you? Off cruising with some trollop!'

'Now, sweetheart. . .'

'*Don't* you sweetheart me,' she commanded, knocking aside his placating hand. 'I've been waiting here on this damn dockside for the past hour, just to make sure I catch you. . .' The voices were finally muffled as the couple climbed into the car.

So Anthea had her wish. Now there was nothing to stop her chasing after Matt as much as she liked. And she had certainly seized the opportunity, linking her arm through his and engaging him in what seemed to be a very intimate conversation as they strolled back along the sea-front.

Caroline hung back, watching them covertly. He was still wearing his evening-clothes, the white dinner-jacket slung casually over his shoulder as he strolled along. Why was it that men could look so interestingly decadent when they had obviously been up all night, while women just looked left over and tacky, their beads and sequins pathetically trying to rival the sun?

She really ought to leave him to Anthea—it would be far safer. But it wasn't going to be easy— an almost murderous jealousy was burning into her heart.

Back at the hotel, she took a shower and went to bed. She was very tired, but it was hard to sleep, and she tossed and turned for hours. By lunchtime she didn't feel at all rested, but she didn't want to stay in bed any longer. Maybe it would be better to go down to the beach.

It was no surprise that Matt was there. He was with Anthea and a noisy bunch of her friends. Caroline found a spare sun-lounger near the back of the beach, and lay down, doing her best to ignore him. She closed her eyes, and let herself doze—strangely, it was easier to sleep out here, in spite of the noise.

She woke to the oddest sensation, and opened her eyes to find Matt's laughing face above her. He was trickling a handful of the soft, warm sand into her navel. She gasped in protest and sat up quickly.

'Hi there, sleepy head,' he greeted her. 'Come on, get that lazy body moving—we're one short of a team for volley-ball.'

She glared at him indignantly. 'I don't want to play volley——'

But he grabbed her hand, and pulled her ruthlessly to her feet. 'Come or —a bit of exercise will cure your hangover in no time.'

'I haven't got a hangover.'

'Well, it'll do you good, anyway. Don't argue.' He helped her on her way with an intimate little pat on her backside, and she flashed him a fulminating glare, but he returned her only one of those mocking smiles.

Anthea was clutching a big red beach-ball, and loudly directing the division of her friends into two teams. 'No, Scott, Ah want you on *my* team,' she was insisting pettishly. 'It ain't fair if Nancy has all the best men!'

That clinched it—why should *she* be the one to leave the field? She'd show the silly girl, quite unmistakably, that she could have Matt if she wanted him. *Then* she'd step aside, and leave Anthea to her hollow victory.

The afternoon was quite a success—the rivalry between the two girls was strong, but on the whole Caroline felt she had got slightly the better of it. Anthea had evidently come to the same opinion, if her growing hostility was anything to go by.

But she wasn't ready to give up yet. 'Hey, Ah just thought of the greatest idea,' she announced to the group in general, but Matt in particular. 'Why don't we all go over to Villefranche for dinner? It's so quaint—you can sit right out by the harbour, and they bring the fish straight off the boats and cook it right there at your table!'

'Sounds good,' agreed Matt readily. 'Caro?'

She nodded, meeting Anthea's ice-blue glare with her most honeyed smile. 'It sounds a lovely idea.'

'Great,' glittered Anthea, smiling like a crocodile. She turned the full kilowatt power of her eyes on Matt. 'Why don't we all meet up at your hotel in a couple of hours, then?' she purred. She touched her hand to his chest. 'See you later.'

Caroline gave considerable thought to what she would wear. She tried on nearly every dress she had brought with her, but none of them seemed quite right. She wanted a complete change of image—Matt's words in the casino still rankled. If he thought she was boring, she'd give him a shock tonight!

In the end, she decided not to wear a dress at all, but a pair of black velvet trousers. And with them she wore a short waistcoat, deep wine red and encrusted with shimmering beads. Usually she would wear a silk blouse underneath it, but tonight she felt like being a little daring.

It looked good. As she moved the waistcoat revealed an inch or two of slim brown midriff, and the occasional tantalising glimpse of her navel. She drew her hair up on to the crown of her head, and let it hang down her back in one thick, glossy tail, then carefully made up her face, emphasising her eyes with a shimmer of bronze shadow, and glossing her lips with pale pink.

As she rode down in the lift to the ground floor, she studied her reflection in the steel doors. Had she gone a little too far, perhaps? She knew a fleeting impulse to press the button and go back upstairs again, to stay in for the evening on her own—her parents had gone off to another party with some friends. But the lift stopped, the doors slid open and, taking a deep, steadying breath, she stepped out into the foyer.

Matt's reaction was everything she could have wished for. He was at the bar, with Anthea at his side, but as Caroline walked towards him he glanced up, and his mouth pursed into a silent whistle of approval. She returned him a cool smile, and accepted the bar-stool he vacated for her.

'Would you like a drink?' he asked, hardly able to take his eyes off her.

'Thank you—I'll have a white wine spritzer,' she responded, delighted with the knowledge that Anthea was turning puce with jealousy. Several of the other young men present were also slanting her very flattering looks—it was an unfamiliar but very heady experience.

It was already quite late when they set off in a noisy cavalcade of cars to drive along the fast autoroute to Nice, and then on round the coast road to the pretty little fishing village of Ville-franche. The place was a delight—a jumble of yellow and pink-stuccoed houses with red pantiled roofs clinging to the steep hillsides above the tiny harbour, fascinating little alleyways and flights of steps that begged to be explored, and a tranquil bay slumbering between the quiet tree-clad slopes of Mt Boron and Cap Ferrat.

They found a charming restaurant, where they could sit outside almost at the edge of the water. The food was excellent—fish, of course—washed down with a light, fresh Lirac rosé that came as quite a surprise to Caroline, who had never tried a rosé before; she tended to stick to the certainty of a good Burgundy or claret.

Anthea was at the top of her form, flirting with every male in sight. It was patently obvious that she was trying to make Matt jealous. She didn't seem to be succeeding—he was watching her with benign amusement, as if he knew perfectly well that he had only to snap his fingers and he could do whatever he liked with her.

Caroline found herself watching him carefully, counting the number of times he smiled at Anthea or spoke to her, comparing it with the amount of attention she was receiving from him herself. She knew she was being ridiculous, but she couldn't help it.

The lively party lingered for a long time over their meal, many of them getting more than a little drunk. It was after midnight when they finally piled back into the cars to drive home.

But Anthea was still in exuberant mood. 'Hey, listen, everybody,' she announced as they reached Cannes, 'it's not even one o'clock—we can't call it a night yet! Why don't we stop off at the club?' There was vociferous agreement from everyone, and she smiled smugly at Caroline. 'Ah don't suppose *you'll* want to come, though, will you, honey?' she enquired in saccharine tones. 'Those sort of places just ain't really your scene, are they?'

Caroline felt stung—had she really sounded so supercilious? No wonder Matt was attracted to Anthea; it was her own fault—by contrast to her own vinegary manner, the bubbly blonde must seem like champagne. If she was going to compete, she was going to have to loosen up a little.

'Of course I'd like to come,' she returned, forcing a smile. 'I only meant that I don't go to nightclubs very often, not that I don't like them at all.' Which was a lie, but she wasn't going to go tamely home to bed and let Anthea have things all her own way.

The nightclub was like the inside of some alien space-ship, all mirrors and glittering steel, coloured spotlights and revolving laser beams that made Caroline feel dizzy. The music was so loud, you could feel it vibrating in the humid air, and the dance-floor was packed.

But she was smiling and laughing as if she had never enjoyed herself so much in her life. Everyone seemed to want to dance with her. They were playing the sort of music you couldn't help dancing to, and she let her slim body sway with the rhythm, teasing her partners like a houri with fleeting glimpses of her slim, tanned midriff.

And suddenly Matt was there, cutting out her current partner without a word of excuse. 'Hey, Miss Kosek, are you planning to start a riot this evening?' he enquired teasingly.

She slanted him a glance of provocative innocence. 'Whatever do you mean?' she purred.

'You have got just about the sexiest navel I've ever seen,' he told her, sliding his arm around her waist and smiling down into her eyes.

He drew her close against him, but she didn't object. She lifted her arms and wrapped them around his neck, letting him move her to the music. She didn't know where Anthea had gone, and she didn't care. *She* was winning now—he wanted to be with *her*. A wild excitement was flooding her veins, more intoxicating than champagne, driving out all rational thought.

The music had changed to something slow and sultry, and she closed her eyes as he leaned his cheek against her hair. The whole length of her body was curved intimately against his, as if she had already surrendered to the fierce male hunger she could sense in his embrace. She was floating, outside time, no past, no future, no one else in the world but the two of them.

She wasn't aware that she had agreed to anything, but somehow she found herself leaving the club with Matt. They wandered down to the sea-front and took off their shoes, then ambled along at the very edge of the wavelets, wrapped up in each other's arms.

'Mmm.' He had found a place in the hollow of her throat that was exquisitely sensitive, and was filling it with hot kisses. 'Your skin tastes delicious.'

She threw her head back, gurgling with delight. She felt crazy, reckless, as if she were on a spinning carousel. The lights along the bay were as bright as a fairground. She wasn't drunk—at least, not with alcohol. The glass and a half of wine she had drunk could not have produced this dizzy elation.

They were dancing in the warm sand, holding hands and spinning each other round, laughing like children. As they drew opposite the hotel, Matt scooped her up in his arms and carried her all the way up the steps, across the road and into the hotel.

The night porter didn't seem to find anything at all unusual in their behaviour, handing over their keys and wishing them a lugubrious goodnight. Matt carried her into the lift, only setting her on her feet when they reached the door of her suite.

'Well, here we are,' she announced breathlessly.

He smiled down at her, his thoughts burning in his eyes. 'Yes, here we are.'

She drew a deep breath, knowing only that she wanted him to stay with her a little longer. If she let him go now, he might go back to Anthea. 'Would you. . .would you like a drink?' she asked.

That slow smile curved his sensuous mouth. 'Thank you,' he responded huskily.

She unlocked the door and flicked the light switch. As he followed her into the room he turned the dimmer down, leaving just a soft glow. There wasn't a sound—her parents weren't back yet from their party.

She turned to him, a quivering tension almost stopping her heart. 'Well. . .I. . .'

He drew her straight into his arms, and his mouth claimed hers in a kiss that was the ultimate temptation. Her mind was a whirlpool of dizzying response as he curved her body to his, melting her bones in the heat of his embrace.

She wasn't aware of being lifted from the ground again, wasn't aware that he had carried her into her bedroom, until he set her down on the bed. Then, for an instant he seemed to hesitate, a question in his eyes. But it wasn't the cool, sensible Miss Kosek who was in control now—some wicked, wanton creature had taken over her body. She smiled up at him invitingly, stretching like a cat.

Matt laughed softly. 'That is *definitely* the sexiest navel I've ever seen,' he murmured, sitting down on the bed beside her and putting out his hand to trace a tantalising circle around it with the very tip of his finger. 'From now on, every time I see you in court in your wig and gown, I'm going to be remembering that navel. It could prove very distracting.'

Dimly Caroline realised that she been afraid of that herself, but as he bent his head over her stomach to swirl his languorous tongue into the sensitive dimple she felt a tide of pure sensuality flood through her, sweeping away any last hope of resistance.

He lifted his head, and his eyes gleamed with anticipation as he reached out his hands to unfasten the bottom button of her waistcoat. She waited, her breath warm on her lips, as his hands moved up, very slowly, unfastening each button in turn.

'Beautiful.' Her heart was racing as he looked down at her. He found the front clasp of her white lace bra, and deftly unclipped it. 'Beautiful,' he murmured again, his hungry gaze caressing her naked curves, making her skin flame with heat.

His two hands slid smoothly up over her soft skin to cup each aching breast as if it were a ripe peach. The tender rose-pink nipples responded, hardening into exquisitely sensitive buds. He laughed huskily, teasing each with the pad of his thumb.

A honeyed tide of languid warmth flowed through her, settling low in her body, hinting at a fierce pleasure she couldn't even imagine. Matt drew her up into his arms, his mouth closing over hers, and she parted her lips in willing surrender.

His kiss was an act of pure possession, long and deep, plundering every sweet corner of her mouth in warning of the possession to come. He had unfastened his shirt, crushing her tender breasts against the rough, hard wall of his chest, and the heat of flesh against flesh inflamed them both.

All her senses were heightened, touch and taste and smell, but her vision was darkened and she could hear only the ragged drag of their breathing, the pounding rhythm of her own heart.

His hot mouth moved on to explore the delicate shell of her ear, trailing down the vulnerable column of her throat to dust scorching kisses over the firm swell of her breasts. Every touch of his lips seemed to brand her bare skin, sending shivers of electric shock through her, and she moved beneath him, her spine curving in languorous pleasure, catching her breath on a sob, trembling as his scalding tongue lapped delicately at one exquisitely sensitive nipple.

He had worked his sorcery on her body, making her his plaything, but she didn't care. She was clinging to him, drowning in sensation, her body on fire. She didn't even notice that he had unzipped her velvet trousers until she felt his hand slide inside her tiny lace briefs, seeking the most intimate caresses. Fleetingly she realised that she should have raised some objection, but already it was far too late. The touch of his fingers was like magic, dissolving her in a warm flood of pure pleasure.

He lifted her in his arms, and before she had realised what was happening he had stripped off both her trousers and her briefs at once, leaving her completely naked. With a flutter of panic she realised that she ought to do something, stop him somehow. But as he rolled off the bed and stood up to take off his own trousers she gazed up at his strong male body, and she couldn't utter a word.

He came back to her, pinning her beneath his weight. Now there was a dangerous urgency in him that didn't recognise her nervous hesitation. His hands were almost rough as they caressed her, his mouth was crushing hers. She felt a little frightened, but a deep, primeval instinct, as old as time, was forcing her submission, and she offered no resistance as he coaxed apart her slim thighs.

She couldn't suppress the sharp gasp that broke from her lips as he took her. He stared down at her in astonishment, but it was far too late to turn back now. She loved him, every part of her belonged to him. She drew him down to her, moving beneath him in surrender, and there was no way he could restrain the driving power inside him.

He thrust into her, and that brief initial pain was forgotten in the rapture of belonging to him totally. His body was slicked with sweat, and the hard muscles of his back moved smoothly under her hands. She responded instinctively, offering her body to the pounding rhythm of his, submerged in the fierce tempest of his desire until with a low, shuddering groan he collapsed into her arms, exhausted.

Afterwards he held her close in his arms as their racing hearts slowly returned to normal. She didn't want to talk, not yet, didn't want to discusss what had happened or why, so she kept her eyes closed and pretended to be asleep. The musky male scent of his body was filling her senses, and in spite of everything she felt a deep sense of contentment.

Carefully Matt shifted his weight, moving her into a more comfortable position. For one awful moment she thought he might be leaving her, but he cradled her head gently against his shoulder, and she felt him rest his cheek against her hair. And slowly the waves of true sleep washed over her.

CHAPTER SIX

CAROLINE woke with a start to the sound of her mother's wailing voice in the next room. It came as a shock to find herself in bed naked, with Matt Farrar beside her. As memory flooded back, her cheeks flamed scarlet, and she jumped up quickly as Matt grunted awake.

'What's going on?' he asked, frowning at her as she quickly wrapped her cotton dressing-gown around her body.

'I'm just going to see,' she muttered, and fled from the room.

The scene that met her eyes could have been re-compiled from the out-takes of a hundred scenes that had gone before it. Her mother was in the middle of the room, sobbing hysterically, her father was waving his arms around and ranting at the top of his voice.

'You've gone too far this time,' her mother was crying. 'Lord knows how much I've stood. But to come back and find you with *her*. . .!' She pointed an accusing finger at the bit-player in this particular episode, who was standing stage left, looking a little stunned.

'She was feeling a bit poorly, so I brought her home,' Adam Kosek insisted with a masterly display of righteous indignation. 'I brought her in here just to give her a little drop of brandy before she went to bed. What do you suggest I should have done? Left her to throw up all over the party?'

'Why should *you* be the one to bring her home?' Betty protested through a soaking wet handkerchief. 'What was it to do with you?'

Caroline hurried forward to intervene, putting a coaxing arm around her mother's sagging shoulders. 'Come on, Mum. Why don't you come into the bedroom and sit down?' she pleaded. 'You don't want to wake everyone in the hotel.'

She had already succeeded in doing that. Several people had gathered outside the open door, some in their night-clothes, to see what was going on. As Caroline coaxed her mother into the other bedroom she saw Matt firmly close the door in their faces. He was dressed now, and fortunately neither of her parents seemed to have noticed which room he had come from.

She settled her mother in one of the armchairs, and glanced up at her father with a weary smile as he hovered in the doorway 'Look, Dad, why don't you go and get her a brandy?' she suggested. 'She'll be all right in a little while.'

He looked relieved at being able to escape. 'Good idea,' he agreed readily. 'Shan't be a tick.' He darted out of the room, and she heard him outside trying to calm his lady-friend, who also seemed to be on the edge of hysterics.

Matt closed the door quietly on the scene. Caroline took a deep breath and faced him. 'Look, I. . .I'm sorry, I'm going to be tied up here for quite a while,' she managed to say.

'Do you need any help?'

'No, no. Please, just. . .I'll. . .see you in the morning.'

'All right.' He drew her gently into his arms, and held her head against his shoulder, gently massaging her scalp with the tips of his fingers.

For a moment she let herself relax against him, but then she pushed him resolutely away. 'G. . .goodnight,' she mumbled, not able to look up at him as she closed the door. She couldn't even let herself think about what had happened— it was fortunate that her parents' crisis looked as if it would absorb all her attention for what remained of the night.

Betty Kosek was sobbing bitterly. 'This really is the last straw,' she insisted in a tear-choked voice. 'This time I'm going to leave him. I mean it, Caro— it's no good you trying to persuade me. I've taken all I'm going to take from that man!' She reached for her daughter's hand and clung to it. 'We're going home, right this minute,' she declared, rising unsteadily to her feet. 'Help me pack, darling. We can get a taxi to the airport.'

There was no force on earth that could have persuaded Betty Kosek to stay in Cannes once she had made up her mind to go. She began dragging clothes out of the wardrobe and bundling them anyhow into a suitcase, all the time fuelling her anger by reciting to herself all the things her husband had done over the years of their marriage, like a litany.

Caroline watched her, bemused and exhausted. She was going to have to go with her—there was no way she was going to be able to manage on her

own. And perhaps it was for the best if she did—
she couldn't face Matt again, not after tonight.

'I'll go and get my own things,' she said. 'I won't
be long.'

She hurried back to her own room, and grabbed
a T-shirt and a pair of jeans to put on. Then she
hauled her suitcase out from the bottom of the
wardrobe and began to pack, as quickly as her
mother but rather more neatly. When Matt
appeared in the doorway she ignored him, continuing with her task.

'What are you doing?' he asked.

'Packing.'

'I can see that. Why are you packing?'

'I'm taking my mother home,' she explained
tensely. She shook back her hair and stood up to
face him.

'I'll come with you,' he offered.

'No, thank you. I'd really rather you didn't,' she
responded, her voice as cold and distant as the
North Pole as she shut her suitcase and picked up
her jacket. 'Excuse me, please,' she said politely,
waiting for him to move out of the doorway.

It was evident that he was taken aback by her
sudden turn-around. 'You're going?' he
demanded sharply. 'Just like that? Without so
much as a goodbye?'

'Goodbye,' she conceded minimally, praying
that he would hurry up and let her go before her
resolve crumbled.

'If I hadn't hung around, you'd just have disappeared, wouldn't you? After what just happened?'

Caroline lifted one enquiring eyebrow. 'What
just happened?' she repeated, her mind numbly

refusing to acknowledge that the vivid memory was real.

He laughed with grating sarcasm. 'All right—I imagined it all. I must have had too much wine,' he conceded, standing aside. 'I should have known better than to think the prudish Miss Kosek could make love like that!'

She stalked past him, her head held high, her spine a rod of ice. She dumped her case on the floor in the main room and went to see what her mother was doing. Behind her she heard the door of the suite slam viciously. For one awful moment she wanted to turn round and run after him. But then she heard her parents' voices, raised in quarrelling again, and with a rueful sigh she pushed open the door of their room, ready to referee.

It was with very mixed feelings that Caroline walked up through Temple Gardens the following week. It would be a relief to get back to work, and have something to fill her mind apart from her own troubles. Her mother had filed for divorce—this would be the third or fourth time she had done it—and her father, terrified of the publicity, had rushed back from Cannes to try to plead with her to change her mind.

Caroline had been caught in the middle of it. Both of them had been prepared to use her unscrupulously, and she was exhausted with listening to them each repeating and repeating their own justifications. One thing she was absolutely sure of— she was never, ever going to risk putting herself in the same position as her mother. She was never going to let love make a fool of her.

It was going to be very hard to face Matthew Farrar-Reid, but it was something she was just going to have to grit her teeth and get over. She knew that he had been due back at work several days earlier—she just hoped he hadn't been boasting about adding her to his long list of conquests!

But to her relief Hugh greeted her with all his usual friendly respect. 'Hello, Caroline. You're looking very well. Did you have a nice holiday?'

'Yes, thank you, Hugh,' she responded blithely. 'Very nice.'

'You look as if you had some good weather, anyway,' he remarked.

'Yes, we did. Haven't you got anything for me?' she added, noting with some surprise that the old-fashioned mantelpiece where the tenants' post and briefs were usually left was empty.

'It's all in the new pigeonholes,' Hugh told her proudly.

She lifted one eyebrow in amused enquiry. 'Pigeonholes, eh? We *are* getting efficient! One of these days we might even get something done about that awful lino on the stairs.'

'If you'd like to raise it at Chambers meeting?' suggested Hugh.

Caroline laughed. 'Nothing will be done until someone breaks their neck,' she prophesied grimly. 'No one wants to fork out a few bob to make this place decent.'

She passed Ralph Easton on the stairs, and he too greeted her cheerfully. 'Ho there! Good to see you back—this place has sadly lacked your feminine charm these past couple of weeks.'

'Good morning, Ralph,' she responded with a smile. 'How's crime?'

'Showing no signs of drying up, thank goodness,' he assured her.

'Glad to hear it.' She spoke lightly, aware by a kind of instinct that Matt was standing just inside the half-open door of Sir Arthur's office. She hurried on up the stairs to her own office, and closed the door with a breath of relief. At least she had got the first hurdle over, and that had bolstered her confidence a little for when she actually had to meet Matt.

But she had barely had time to sit down at her desk when there was a peremptory rap on the door, and Matt himself walked in. She glanced up at him, struggling to maintain her mask of composure. He seemed to dwarf her small office, and the cool mockery in his eyes was unnerving.

'Good morning,' she greeted him with formal politeness, shuffling papers, hinting that she was very busy.

'Welcome back,' he responded, an inflection of sardonic humour in his voice.

'Thank you,' she conceded, her tone and expression discouraging any further intrusion.

He leaned casually against the frame of the door as if he was in no hurry to go. 'Afraid to come out of your box again, Miss Kosek?' he taunted softly.

She drew a deep, steadying breath. 'Whatever. . .may have happened between us. . .' she ignored his mocking laugh, 'I would prefer that it should be forgotten.'

Matt shook his head. 'I'm sorry, I can't do that,' he murmured provocatively. 'I told you, every time I look at you, I can't help remembering that deliciously sexy navel of yours.'

Caroline felt her cheeks flush a heated red. 'Look, just. . .go away, leave me alone,' she muttered. 'I don't even want to think about it.'

'Why not?' He closed the door, and came towards her. 'You seemed to be enjoying it at the time. Why are you acting now as if it was something to be ashamed of?' He perched on the edge of her desk, and brushed his fingers lightly over her cheek.

She jerked her head away sharply. 'Don't!'

He sighed, and caught her shoulders in a firm grip, turning her to face him. 'I should never have let you run away like that,' he said. 'I should have made you leave your parents to sort out their own problems. Now I'm going to have to start all over again.'

He bent towards her, his intent unmistakable. Panic infused her brain, and gathering every shred of will-power she possessed she pushed her chair sharply back from the desk. 'I said leave me alone!' she snarled furiously. 'If you touch me again, I'll. . .'

His slow smile mocked her. 'You'll do what? Charge me with sexual harassment? You wouldn't have much of a case. "*Volenti non fit injuria*—no wrong can be done to one who consents".'

'I am *not* consenting,' she grated through clenched teeth. 'Not now, not ever.'

Matt raised one quizzical eyebrow. 'No? That night in Cannes. . .'

'I was drunk,' she lied desperately.

He hesitated, his brows snapping together. 'Drunk? You didn't seem very drunk.'

She laughed derisively. 'Oh, I'm sure it appeals to your ego to pretend it isn't true,' she sneered. 'But I can assure you, I certainly wouldn't have gone to bed with you if I'd been sober.' An angry light was kindling in his eyes, and she concluded recklessly, 'So congratulations—you won your bet. But only by taking advantage of me.'

He froze. 'I see.' He rose to his feet, his hard mouth twisting into a cold sneer. 'Well, rest assured, it won't happen again,' he rapped harshly, and, turning on his heel, he strode from the room.

Caroline leaned back weakly in her seat and closed her eyes. A single tear trickled slowly down her cheek. She had made very sure that he wouldn't approach her again—in fact she had probably ensured that he would hate her forever.

The next weeks were very busy. Caroline had a number of important cases coming up, and had little time to dwell on her personal problems. Matt virtually ignored her, and when he was forced to acknowledge her his behaviour was distant and formal. And that was what she wanted. . .wasn't it?

But as the weeks passed she grew more and more tense. *Surely* she couldn't be. . .pregnant? No, it wasn't possible. It was so unfair—to be punished like that for one tiny mistake. Maybe it was just the fact that she was worrying about it. If she could just relax, stop glancing at the calendar every five minutes, nature would take its course.

But she couldn't relax. Suddenly, everywhere she looked, there seemed to be pregnant women—in the streets, on the underground train, on every jury. . .What would everyone say? There was no way she would be able to keep a thing like that a secret—she could just imagine herself standing up in court, vainly trying to hide her growing bulge in the folds of her stuff gown.

Oh, how they would all laugh at her behind their hands. Her, the frosty Miss Kosek, the Iron Maiden, about to become an unmarried mother. The career she had struggled so hard to establish would be wrecked beyond repair—who would ever trust a barrister who couldn't even manage her own private life properly?

Stop it, she scolded herself over and over. A little calm common sense was what was needed. The first thing to do was find out if she really was pregnant. There were those little home-testing kits she had seen advertised in magazines—she would get one today. Once she knew for certain, then she could think about what to do.

For some stupid reason she didn't want to go into a chemist's either near home or near the Temple, afraid that she might be spotted by someone she knew. So she left the Tube station at Earl's Court, and went into a shop there. Even so, she felt embarrassed, trying to smile as if she was eagerly anticipating happy news and clumsily hiding her ringless left hand.

She read the instructions very carefully before she went to bed, and woke early to give herself plenty of time to do the test. Her heart was in her mouth as she waited for the result. It was positive.

Impatiently she swept the lot into the rubbish bin. 'Damn stupid thing,' she muttered angrily to herself. 'How can you expect a thing like that to work?'

Maybe she had made a mistake with the instructions. Maybe the results weren't very reliable—it must have been a false reading. She would try again tomorrow—but this time she would get several different sorts of kit, to give herself every chance of getting it right.

She bought four, and they all gave the same result. Positive.

Caroline stared at her pale face in the bathroom mirror. Thoughts of her ruined career, of the scorn of her colleagues, faded into insignficance beside the one thought that seared her brain. Matt. If she had made him angry, he certainly had his revenge now. She could almost see the mockery in those blue eyes, the sneering smile on that hard, arrogant mouth. No, no, she couldn't face him, she couldn't bear him to know what he had done to her.

There was only one solution. She couldn't go through with this pregnancy. She was going to have to do something—and soon. She didn't have much time. Her mind recoiled in horror from what she was planning to do, but some kind of dark determination took over.

There were plenty of advertisements on the Tube station—everywhere she looked they seemed to jump out at her in black and white. She tried not to look as if she was memorising the telephone number, and she didn't write it down until she got to her office.

She wasn't in court today, thank goodness, and she had no appointments straight after lunch. She could go today—the sooner the better. Her hand was shaking as she dialled.

All morning she buried herself in her work, trying not to think about what she was going to do. Any niggling doubts were instantly quelled by the thought of Matt's mocking blue eyes. She didn't feel like eating any lunch. It was a gloriously sunny day, almost an insult to her desolate mood.

The clock ticked away the time with remorseless precision, and at a quarter past one she picked up her handbag and left the office. The clinic was a bus ride away. She found a seat near the back of the bus, and sat staring out unseeingly at the passing streets.

After several stops the man next to her rose to get off, and as she slid over towards the window a young woman sat down next to her—a young woman with a baby in her arms. Caroline tried hard not to look. The mother was murmuring softly to the child, who was gurgling content-edly—the two of them seemed to be in a loving world of their very own, oblivious of everything around them.

She couldn't resist one quick glance. A pretty pink face was peeping out from the folds of a white, hand knitted shawl, one tiny perfect fist with the most delicate little fingernails gripped a fold of the wool. . .Caroline felt her heart contract.

A baby. She had been refusing to let herself think of her condition in terms of expecting a baby. It had been a pregnancy—something unpleasant she had caught, like a dose of measles. Something for which there was a straightforward cure. . .

She stood up quickly, with a breathless, 'Excuse me.' The girl moved out of the way, and she stumbled somehow down the bus and got off at the next stop. One or two people glanced at her, as if wondering if she were ill, but she walked away quickly, losing herself in the shopping crowds.

Everywhere there seemed to be infants and toddlers, shops full of prams and teddy-bears. She wandered into one, and found herself standing by a wicker crib, lined with dainty white cotton lawn. A baby. . .her baby, Matt's baby. With his nose, his light brown hair, his blue eyes. Matt's baby—all she would ever have of him. A baby she could love as she never dared let herself love him.

'Can I help you?'

She looked up, startled out of her reverie. A shop assistant was standing there, smiling politely. 'Oh. . .no, I was just browsing,' she stammered.

The girl nodded. 'Of course. This is one of our most popular cots—it's pretty, isn't it?'

'Yes, it is. But. . .I think I'd prefer something a bit less frilly.'

'Of course. Well, we've got the drop-sided type of cot—they're a little more practical. The baby would grow out of this one rather quickly. Would you prefer plain wood, or this sort?' She indicated a white-painted one, with a soft-focus stencil of Peter Rabbit on the headboard.

'That's nice,' Caroline agreed. She laughed

rather nervously. 'It's probably a bit silly buying it so soon, it isn't due for ages yet, but. . .'

The shop assistant smiled with womanly understanding. 'Well, you don't want to leave it all until the last minute, do you? We've got a quilt and a set of cot-bumpers to match this one, if you'd like to have a look at them.'

'Thank you.' Caroline took a deep breath. She wasn't quite sure of the moment when she had changed her mind, but she knew now that she wasn't going to the clinic. 'Can you deliver the goods if I buy them today?'

'Of course,' the girl assured her. 'There's no charge within the London area.'

She rode back on the crowded bus, feeling as if she were floating on air. Total strangers smiled at her, as if sensing the elation that was surging inside her. She wanted to tell them all, wanted to shout it from the rooftops. *I'm going to have a baby.*

What would it be—a boy or a girl? It didn't matter. A boy would be thrilling—a son, to grow up taller than her, to tease her with 'Oh, Mum!' when she scolded him for getting into trouble at school. A girl would be fun, dressing her up in tough-guy little dungarees and watching her play with her dolls.

Steady, Caroline, she reminded herself severely. She had a lot to think about, decisions to make. Chiefly, what was she going to do about her career? It wouldn't be easy to keep on working, in the face of all the gossip and speculation. And after it was born. . .Oh, but she would manage somehow.

Her mother would be shocked, of course, but she would soon get over the disappointment of missing a wedding in the excitement of preparing for her grandchild. And her father—he would only be concerned with the harm it might do to his image to be a grandfather, and that would be the same whether she was married or not.

And she would have to tell Matt, sooner or later. She bit her lip. It wasn't going to be easy to face him. Acknowledging to herself that she was carrying his baby made her emotions feel even more vulnerable towards him, and she knew that as her pregnancy progressed, as her body changed to accommodate the new life that was growing inside her, all her instincts would make her want to depend on the man who had fathered her child.

But she couldn't do that. That was exactly what her mother had done, and what a bitter price she had paid for it. No, at all costs she must resist the temptation to cling to him. She would just let the information out coolly, along with the assertion that all the responsibility was hers, and she neither needed nor wanted any help from him.

The bus reached the stop outside the imposing façade of the Royal Courts of Justice in the Strand. She alighted, and took a few deep, steadying breaths before crossing the road and passing under the ancient archway into Middle Temple Lane.

She wouldn't tell anyone yet, not even Matt. It would be another couple of months before anything began to show, and that would be soon enough. By then she might have worked out some strategy for dealing with the situation. Hugh seemed to notice nothing unusual about her as she

breezed past him and hurried upstairs to her
office.

As she pushed open the door, she caught her
breath in shock. Matt was sitting at her desk, and
his face was grim. 'Come in,' he invited.

She returned him a frosty glare. 'Thank you,'
she responded tartly, watching him warily. 'This
is my office, after all.'

'You'd better shut the door,' he went on in the
same taut voice.

A sudden chill gripped her heart, and she sank
into the chair she usually offered to clients. He
knew—but *how*? Her eyes focused on the big white
blotter on her desk, and all the colour seemed to
drain from her face. She had written down the
telephone number of the clinic, and the time of her
appointment.

'You've been spying on me,' she accused him
furiously.

'Not at all. If you recall, I'm representing your
client's co-defendant in the Tilbury cocaine smuggling. The prosecution are requesting an urgent
conference, and I needed to get in touch with you.'
And so of course he had tried the number on the
blotter—and reached the clinic. 'I can see from
your face that my first assumption was correct.
Why the hell didn't you tell me about it?'

'Because it's none of your business,' she
retorted, instinctively on the defensive.

'Oh, come on,' he rapped harshly. 'You may
have been drunk that night in Cannes, but I
wasn't. I knew you were a virgin. Are you trying
to tell me that after twenty-seven years of chastity
you ran straight out and threw your cap over the

windmill with every Tom, Dick and Harry in town?'

Caroline felt her cheeks flame scarlet. 'No, of course not!' she protested furiously.

'Then I think this *is* my business, don't you?'

'No, I do not,' she retorted. 'I'm not asking anything from you.'

'Don't you think I have some right to have a say in your decision?'

'No.' She glowered at him in cold fury. She hadn't wanted it to be like this—but she had no intention of letting him think he could bully her. 'If you're so concerned about the welfare of your progeny, perhaps you should be a little more careful how you sow your wild oats!'

Matt drew in a deep breath, as if he was having difficulty controlling his temper. 'I would have been, if I'd known. And of course, I wasn't expecting to win my bet quite so easily,' he added insultingly.

Caroline felt her fingers curl into claws. 'You. . .' She couldn't think of anything bad enough to call him.

He shook his head, holding up a placating hand. 'I'm sorry—that was uncalled for,' he apologised quickly. 'Anyway, it's too late to cry over spilt milk now. We have to decide what to do about it.'

'*I* have to decide,' she corrected him tersely.

'An abortion?'

She returned him a cool, level look, disdaining to answer.

'Dammit, Caro, you can't!' Abruptly he rose to his feet, and turned to stare out of the window, his hands thrust deep into his pockets. 'Look, we can get married. . .'

It was fortunate that he had his back to her at that moment, and didn't see the effect his words had on her. It was as if she had stepped off a cliff. But she had to hold on to her resolution. 'I. . .I don't think so,' she choked.

His broad shoulders hunched in tension. 'Please don't dismiss the idea so casually,' he grated. 'It's really the best solution.'

'Is it, indeed?' she countered, finding her voice in frosty anger.

'Of course it is.' He turned back to her. 'I don't want you to have an abortion, Caro. *Please*.'

She had opened her mouth to argue, but that last word changed her mind. 'I'm not going to,' she conceded. 'I'd already decided not to go through with it.'

Matt let go his breath in a long sigh, and sank down into the chair. 'Why didn't you say so in the first place?'

'If you hadn't come in here with your demands and your insistence on your rights, I would have done,' she informed him tartly.

He smiled at her—when he smiled like that, it took every ounce of will-power she possessed to resist his magic. 'I'm sorry, Caro, I just. . .Look, I meant what I said, it would be best if we got married.'

She shook her head, fighting to retain a grip on her common sense. 'There's no need for us to do that,' she said firmly. 'I can manage perfectly well on my own.'

'Don't be ridiculous!'

Her eyes flashed a frost warning. 'I don't want to marry you,' she insisted, her voice conveying the unmistakable message that her decision was final. 'Of course you can visit the baby as often as you like, I won't stop you doing that.'

'Oh, thank you. Every other Saturday, an afternoon pushing a pram around the park, with all the other weekend fathers? Well, I'm sorry if it's inconvenient for you, but I do feel a certain responsibility towards my child, and I'd prefer that he wasn't born a nameless bastard.'

Her anger was threatening to explode inside her skull. 'How *dare* you say a thing like that?' she demanded with cold venom.

'It's your damned stupid obstinacy that's forcing the poor brat into that position,' he retaliated.

'He—or she—will have a name. My name. One of the few good things that can be said for the so-called permissive society is that a woman no longer has to pay for the mistake of getting pregnant by marrying a man she can't stand!'

'If you're planning to make the news public,' drawled Matt with cutting sarcasm, 'wouldn't it be better to put an announcement in *The Times*, rather than shouting it from the rooftops?'

She glared at him furiously, but she moderated her tone. 'We have nothing further to discuss,' she said. 'Now, if you don't mind, I am rather busy.'

'We could have dinner tonight.'

'No, we couldn't. Now, will you please go?'

'Caro. . .'

'Then I'll go. I'll be back in fifteen minutes, and I'll expect to find my office empty.'

'Or you'll do what?' he challenged mockingly.

His cool arrogance was more than she could stand. 'If you want to be allowed to see your child,' she enuciated clearly, 'I suggest you try to stay on the good side of me.'

He stared at her, his eyes freezing over. 'I see.' He rose to his feet. 'Very well, you've made your terms clear.' He walked out of the office, closing the door behind him just a little harder than was necessary.

The encounter had left her shaken, and it took her several minutes to recover her equilibrium. Maybe it shouldn't have come as such a surprise to her that he should offer to marry her. If the secret of her child's paternity ever leaked out—which it well might—the scandal could be quite damaging to his career. Those who had looked on his other peccadilloes with a certain amount of amused tolerance would regard this affair in a very different light.

And, of course, there was the matter of family pride. The child would carry the blood-line of the Farrar-Reids. It probably appealed to Matt's sense of dynasty to marry and produce a son and heir. A small shiver ran down the length of her spine. Once he had backed himself to get her into bed in less than two weeks. He had succeeded in about as many days. If he had really made up his mind that he was going to marry her. . .

CHAPTER SEVEN

THE solution to Caroline's difficulties came unexpectedly. On Sunday she went over to have lunch with her parents, as usual. She had been rehearsing for days how she was going to break her news to them, but the minute she arrived she saw that they had some exciting news for her.

'Oh, Caro, you'll never guess!' her mother blurted out excitedly. 'Your father's been offered a starring role in *Mandate*. Isn't it marvellous?'

'Marvellous,' she agreed, with rather less than her mother's enthusiasm. She rarely watched television, and the only time she had seen the glitzy soap opera it had seemed to consist of nothing but surly men and simpering women.

'I'll be playing Lorne McCord's English half-brother, Chester,' Adam Kosek explained, his voice and features taking on a subtle change as he fell into role. 'When I first arrive, the family try to claim that I'm illegitimate, but it turns out that Lorne himself is the illegitimate one.'

'Well, well!' murmured Caroline drily.

'We'll be moving to Hollywood,' Betty rushed on. 'It would be simply lovely if you came with us, darling.'

Caroline made a snap decision. 'All right,' she agreed.

She must have spoken so calmly that her mother

didn't even realise what she had said. 'I mean, I know you have your job. . .'

'Oh, I was planning to have some time off anyway.' There was no point in beating about the bush. 'I'm going to have a baby,' she announced bluntly.

Betty blinked at her, not sure if she had heard correctly. 'A. . .a baby? But. . .well, I know that sort of thing's very fashionable these days, but don't you think it would be better if you waited a little while, and got married first?'

Caroline almost smiled. 'I can't wait,' she explained calmly. 'It's due in February.'

'*What*?'

'Don't get hysterical, Mum,' she begged. 'You said yourself, it's very fashionable these days.' Maybe humour wasn't very appropriate in the circumstances, but she didn't want the scene to turn into a melodrama.

'What was that?' her father demanded. 'But. . .well, whose is it?'

'It's mine,' she responded, her voice still calm.

Adam seemed to be in danger of exploding. 'This is no time for your clever answers, young lady,' he roared.

'Oh, I'm sorry, Dad,' she apologised, taking his hand. 'But please don't go mad about it. I'm twenty-seven years old, and I'm not very likely to get married now. I don't have much longer left.'

He relented too, and his voice was much softer. 'Are you saying you planned it?' he asked.

'Not exactly,' she admitted. 'But I am very pleased about it. Say you are too.'

'Well, I don't know. I. . .well, I suppose I won't

be able to go on claiming I'm forty-two any more, will I? What about forty-eight? That's got a nice ring to it, don't you think?'

She laughed, feeling a rush of affection for this vain, shallow man—only Adam Kosek, on being told he was about to become a grandfather, would think first of lying about his age.

Betty had taken her lead from her husband, and the tears in her eyes had turned miraculously to tears of joy. 'Oh, Caro! Oh, darling, I'm so happy!'

Caroline smiled at her. 'Thanks, Mum,' she said, squeezing her hand too. 'Well, so when are we going to Hollywood?'

Victoria Elizabeth Kosek made her debut at six pounds ten ounces, in a sunny bedroom of the big white house on Cielo Drive that her grandfather had leased. She had a head of downy blonde hair, and her eyes were such a vivid blue that they were certainly going to stay that colour. Adam was convinced he could see Kosek features in her squashy little face, but Caroline could detect another very distinct likeness, which she kept to herself. The child was going to be the image of her father.

She wrote to Matt a few days after the birth, enclosing a photograph. Two weeks later a huggable yellow teddy-bear was delivered, together with a chillingly polite note in response to her letter. His reaction came as no surprise—they had parted on the most acrimonious terms. He had been furious when she had told him that she was going to America, but there had been absolutely nothing he could do about it.

She wrote to him regularly after that, sending pictures of Vicky as she grew. The correspondence did nothing to warm their relationship—it was simply a duty. But he never failed to send a little present for Vicky—between her absent father and her doting grandparents she was gathering the biggest collection of soft toys in the world.

Soon after arriving in Los Angeles Caroline had started doing some voluntary work, helping in a legal advice clinic at a Neighborhood Center on the wrong end of Sunset Boulevard, and a few months after the birth she went back there. Sometimes she left Vicky with Maggie, who of course had come out to America with Betty, and sometimes she took her along, wrapped up like a papoose—there were always plenty of eager hands to look after her while she worked.

. Something about the California air must have done strange things to Betty Kosek. When Adam started to stray after one of his young co-stars, instead of sitting at home feeling sorry for herself, as usual, she went off and got herself a face-lift, and soon after that she was frequently seen around town with a man ten years her junior.

When Adam, in a furore of righteous indignation, threatened to divorce her, she accepted the offer with an alacrity that stunned him, took him for a very comfortable divorce settlement, and went off to live happily in New York with her lover.

Meanwhile Adam, not to be outdone, married his young girlfriend, and when falling ratings prompted the network to cancel his show, he accepted an offer from Australian Television to star in a similar series for them, and went off to live in Sydney.

After they had gone, Caroline stayed on in Los Angeles for a while—she took a lease on a comfortable little clapboard house near the beach. She had made some friends, and she enjoyed working at the law centre. And yet as time passed, she knew that she wasn't settled there. She couldn't get a work permit, and she couldn't practise in the American courts. She missed the cloistered gentility of the Inns of Court, the archaic formality of the Old Bailey. She missed her friends in London, she missed the rain. She was homesick.

Vicky grew into a sturdy toddler, with a very definite will of her own, but blessed with such a winning smile that she could melt the hardest heart. Just like her father. She was two years old when Caroline wrote to tell Matt that they were returning to England.

In spite of all her objections, he insisted on meeting them at the airport. And she had to confess, as she struggled through Customs with Vicky asleep in her arms, that it was a relief to knew there was someone there to take over the chore of getting them safely into town.

She wasn't sure how she was going to feel about seeing Matt again. After all, it had been over two years. She ought to be able to face him after all this time without falling to pieces. She had no idea who was sharing his life now. . .who was sharing his bed.

She saw him as soon as she stepped into the arrivals lounge. He appeared to have come straight from court, and was wearing an immaculate pin-striped suit and yellow bowtie. As he walked towards her she took a deep breath—she had almost forgotten the sheer physical impact of his presence. As he drew closer, she could see the cold glint in those steel-blue eyes.

'H. . .hello,' she greeted him, trying to keep her voice steady.

'Hello.' As he let his gaze slide over her, she felt her heart begin to beat a little faster. 'You're looking well,' he remarked, his cool tone depriving his words of any trace of flattery. 'California must have agreed with you.'

'Thank you,' she responded levelly. Of course, the changes that had come slowly would make more of an impact on someone who hadn't seen her for such a long time. Not only was she tanned and healthy, with a few more curves than before, but she wore her hair in a more flattering style now—a loose bun on top of her head, with wispy curls around her face to soften the outline. And she had swapped her thick glasses for contact lenses.

But the biggest change was in her manner. She had absorbed some of the laid-back, easy style of Los Angles. She was more confident now, much less brittle—she could match Matthew Farrar-Reid for self-assurance.

'Well, this is Vicky,' she announced. The child in her arms stirred, but didn't waken.

Matt gazed at his daughter, instantly captivated. 'She. . .she's pretty,' he murmured, an odd little catch in his voice. 'She's so much bigger than I thought she'd be.'

'She *is* two years old,' she reminded him. His

eyes glinted accusingly. He had missed all those very special baby times—the first steps, the first words—times that would never come again. 'Look, we're both very tired,' she said. 'Can we just get going?'

'OK. Is this all your luggage?'

'Yes—I sent the rest on ahead.'

'You're still set on staying in a hotel?'

'Just until I find somewhere to live. The first thing I'm going to do—after I've had a good sleep—is go flat-hunting.'

'And then what?'

'I shall be going back to work, of course.'

'And who's going to look after Vicky?'

'I'm going to get an au pair,' she informed him levelly.

'An au pair?'

'There's no need to sound so shocked,' she retorted, a sting of annoyance in her voice. 'It's a very good agency—my friend recommended it.'

'I see,' he said tersely. 'Well, you made it clear from the beginning that I'm going to have no say in the upbringing of my daughter. Are you at least going to let me see her regularly?'

'Of course. I told you I would.'

'Thank you.' He picked up her two heavy bags as if they weighed nothing at all, and without another word led the way to the buses that served the enormous car parks.

Unlike many single parents, Caroline wasn't short of money, and within a few days she had signed the lease on a garden flat in Barnes, close to where she used to live before she went to America. The au pair agency also proved very efficient, promising to provide her with a girl by the following week.

As soon as she was settled, she put a call through to Sir Arthur. His greeting was most encouraging. 'Why, Caroline, how lovely to hear from you. When did you get back?'

'Just a couple of weeks ago. Could you spare me some time, Sir Arthur?'

'Of course. I hope you're planning to come back to us—you're not to think of taking yourself off to someone else's Chambers, now. We've got a vacancy coming up here, you know,' he added conspiratorially.

'You have?'

'Yes. The word is that Bill Latimer's finally going to get his full-time appointment to the Bench. It's still under wraps, of course, but I had it from Sir Hugh himself—we played a couple of rounds at the club on Sunday.'

Dear old Sir Arthur—he never could resist dropping the names of the High Court judges he played golf with into any conversation. 'I'm glad for him,' she said with sincerity. 'He's waited a long time for it. And I'm glad for myself, too, if it means there'll be a tenancy to let.'

'We'll be very glad to have you,' he assured her. 'There's a Chambers meeting on Friday—I'll raise it then. I don't think you need worry which way the vote will go.'

It had been agreed that Matt was to visit every Saturday afternoon. Once Vicky had got to know him, he would be able to take her out, but for the first few weeks at least Caroline knew she would have to be with them. But she was going to have to get used to his presence, she realised—he had made it perfectly clear that he intended to be a part of his daughter's life. And she was glad of that for Vicky's sake, at least. As she grew up, it would be important for her to have a father around.

She had dressed Vicky up in a brand-new cotton jump-suit, pink, with an appliqué elephant on the front, and brushed the fine gold curls till they shone. She looked scrumptious, like a plump pink cherub in an Italian fresco, but as two o'clock approached she seemed to sense Caroline's edginess, and was becoming increasingly fractious.

As the doorbell rang, Caroline felt that nervous flutter begin again in her heart, felt that strange glow of heat that seemed to spread right through her body. She picked Vicky up and gave her a quick cuddle. 'Please, darling, don't cry now,' she whispered coaxingly. 'Let's see that lovely big smile.'

She took a deep breath and opened the door. Matt was wearing a white shirt, with the collar open and the sleeves rolled back over his strong brown forearms, and a pair of casual jeans. But still he had that oddly compelling presence.

He frowned with anxious concern at the sight of the child's red face. 'What's the matter with her?' he demanded. 'She's not ill, is she?'

Caroline laughed. 'If you'd seen the amount of alphabetti-spaghetti she ate for lunch, you wouldn't even ask,' she assured him, 'Come on in.'

'Oh.' He followed her into the sitting-room, and

produced a brightly wrapped parcel. 'I brought her a present.'

Vicky's eyes brightened as she saw the gift, and she made a grab for it. 'Now say "Ta,"' Caroline prompted her gently.

In a moment the child had been transformed from a little demon into a angel. Her tears dried, and her smile appeared like the sunshine after rain. 'Ta,' she repeated obediently, taking the present eagerly and scrabbling clumsily at the wrapping.

Caroline put her down on the floor, and Matt crouched down beside her, totally absorbed in watching her. In the parcel was a painted wooden pull-along train, with little wooden figures that came out—a fact which she quickly discovered, much to her delight.

Caroline gave an inward sigh of relief as tranquillity was at last restored. 'Would you like a coffee?' she asked Matt.

He glanced up at her, and actually smiled. 'Yes, please.'

She went into the kitchen, and filled the coffee filter. Matt had sat down on the floor, and was quickly making friends with his small daughter, who was chattering away happily to him—not that her speech was very clear yet, but he was responding to her as attentively as if she were making perfect sense. Watching them, Caroline suddenly felt an unexpected pang of guilt for keeping them apart for so long.

It felt strange to see him there, in her flat; strange to recognise the striking resemblance between the two of them—she had always known it was there, but seeing those two faces side by side! No one could ever doubt that he was her father.

Her father. . .The child was a permanent link between them, one she could never escape. And that powerful tug of attraction was still there—the years had done nothing to diminish that. She turned back into the kitchen, instinctively reaching for the glasses she now rarely wore.

She carried the coffee-cups through to the sitting-room, and set them down on a low table. Matt moved to sit in one of the armchairs, still fascinated by Vicky's scientific experimentation into the various possibilities of the pieces of the toy.

'Well, I expect you know by now that the vote at Chambers meeting went in your favour,' he remarked a trifle acidly.

She nodded. 'A unanimous vote?' she pointed out, a question in her voice.

'I was detained elsewhere.'

'How very convenient,' she remarked drily.

'So when are you coming back to work?' he asked, sipping his coffee.

'On Monday,' she told him. The grim set of his face spoke clearer than a thousand words. 'You don't approve?'

He shrugged his wide shoulders. 'Apparently it's none of my business,' he reminded her acidly.

'She won't suffer because I'm working,' she insisted firmly. 'I've got an au pair—Lisle. She's very capable, and Vicky's taken to her right away.' That wasn't strictly true—the plump French girl looked a lot younger than she had expected, and she was very slow. But still, once she got used to being away from home for the first time, living in a foreign country, she would probably be very good.

'But you don't need to work,' Matt argued. 'If you don't want to be dependent on your father, why won't you let me——?'

'No,' she interrupted quickly.

'But she's my child, my responsibility.'

'I'm working because I want to,' she explained, measuring her words carefully. 'I love my job—and, much as I love Vicky, I'd go screaming mad if all I had to do all day was look after her. I know there are a lot of women who could ask for nothing more, but. . .well, would it satisfy you? Not just for a week or two, I mean, but month after month.'

'Well, I. . .' Suddenly he smiled, and shrugged his wide shoulders. 'No, I suppose it would get a little monotonous,' he conceded.

Caroline returned the smile. 'Well, then. The time I do spend with her will be extra precious. I think that will be better for her than having me around all the time, if I'm just getting bored and edgy. Maybe I'm not an ideal mother, but I'll be doing my best.'

'All right,' he agreed. 'But even so, don't you think it would be better for her if we were to get married? You could still carry on working, if that's what you wanted to do.'

She had been half expecting that he would bring that up again, and her answer was well-rehearsed. 'No, I don't think so,' she said evenly. 'I'll never stop you seeing her, I promise. I'm very glad that you want to take such an interest in her. And I hope for her sake that you and I can be friends. But as for any other kind of relationship—no.' She shook her head to add emphasis to her words.

'I see.' There was a certain grimness in his expression that made her doubt that he had accepted her refusal as final, but he had evidently decided not to pursue the matter any further at present. He glanced around the flat for the first time. 'Nice place,' he approved generously.

'Thank you. I was very pleased to get it— particularly with the garden. It'll be lovely for Vicky when the summer comes, and I'm looking forward to planting a few flowers.'

He stood up, and strolled over to the open french windows to look out at the small plot. Vicky followed him, and he scooped her, up, swinging her high in the air and making her squeal with delight. It wasn't long before she had him crawling on the floor on his hands and knees, giving her pony rides.

Caroline laughed. 'She's got you twisted round her little finger already,' she teased him.

'She's gorgeous,' he agreed, trying to defend himself as the child hauled on a fistful of hair. 'Hey, you little monster!' he protested, laughing. 'What are you trying to do to me?' He caught her in a big hug, cuddling her close. 'You know, my father would really love to see her,' he added to Caroline.

She blinked at him in astonishment. 'Your father? But. . .you mean you've told him about her?'

'Of course—she *is* his only grandchild. In fact, I

was hoping you might let me take her down to visit him one weekend.'

Caroline hesitated. She was reluctant to agree, and yet it seemed cruel to deny Matt's father the chance to see the child. 'I. . .I don't know,' she mused. 'She's never been away from me before.'

'Well, you can come too, of course.'

She stared at him. 'What, down to Suffolk—with you?'

Matt smiled with a hint of the sardonic humour she remembered so well. 'Would that be so bad? It would only be for a few days. I though we could go down for the Spring Bank Holiday—the family usually try to all get together then.'

'I. . .I'll need to think about it,' she temporised. 'No, Vicky, don't play with that,' she added quickly as the child picked up a half-empty coffee-cup. 'That's right, sweetheart, give it to Mummy. Thank you.'

The afternoon passed much more enjoyably than Caroline had expected. By the time he left, she had accepted his invitation to spend a week-end at his family home in Suffolk—wryly she had to admit to herself that she was still far too suscep-tible to that persuasive charm of his.

'By the way,' he added as he said goodbye, 'I've got a case you might find interesting, if you'd like to have a look at it on Monday. It's a Third Party Negligence. My client's a charity that runs hostels for vagrants—the claim arises out of a fire that one of the residents started, injuring one of the others.'

'Sounds interesting,' she agreed.

'Right. See you Monday.' He leaned forward

and kissed Vicky's rosy cheek. 'Bye, sweetheart. See you next weekend.'

Sorrow quivered on the toddler's bottom lip as she realised she was losing her 'pony'. She held out her chubby arms to him as he climbed into his car, calling 'Dad-dad.' He waved to her as he drove away, and she waved back until the car disappeared round the corner.

'Come on then, sweetheart,' Caroline murmured when he had gone, 'let's see what we've got for tea, shall we?'

'Caroline! How nice to have you back!'

'Hello, Hugh. It's nice to be back. I hope my presence isn't going to make things too crowded.'

'Not at all,' he assured her. 'We can always make room for the odd squatter or two. You can use your old office—I'm afraid your desk has been taken over, but Bill won't mind you using his. Between you and me, he won't be here much longer. He's destined for higher things.'

'Which is what comes of playing golf with the right people.' Caroline hoped no one had noticed that she had caught her breath at the sound of Matt's voice behind her. 'Hello, Caroline,' he went on easily. 'Welcome back. Maybe if you've got a few minutes this morning you'd step down to my office—that is if you're not above filling in your time with a bit of devilling for your hard-pressed colleagues.'

She laughed, relaxing a little. He was striking just the right note for their relationship—friendly but discreet. 'Of course I'm not,' she assured him.

'I'm afraid it's going to be back to basics for me for a while.'

'I've got a Reckless Driving here,' Hugh put in. 'It's pretty routine stuff, but if you don't mind taking it. . .'

'I'd be delighted.' She held out her hand for the fold of manuscript, and slid the pink ribbon off it to scan the sheets. 'Fine. Anything else?'

'Well, there's a couple of requests for Counsel's Opinion waiting, and I'm expecting a Section 27 Wounding.'

'Send them up,' she invited cheerfully. 'The sooner I get back into court, the better, even if it is only Bow Street Magistrates.'

Matt smiled. 'Oh, I dare say it won't be long before you're back at the Bailey,' he told her. 'The rest of us had better look to our laurels.'

The scruffy old building hadn't changed at all in two years. The worn brown lino on the stairs was still there, the light-bulb on the top landing hadn't been replaced. Such cheeseparing was common to most Chambers of barristers—it wasn't just that they were too mean to vote to pay a little more into the communal maintenance fund. It was almost an affectation, a kind of snobbery—just as they preferred their black stuff gowns to show distinct signs of wear.

She pushed open her office door and looked around with a sigh of contentment. It was just the same as it had always been—except that there were someone else's things on the desk that used to be hers. A woman, to judge from the little personal touches; a suede-covered box for pens and pencils, a flourishing parlour-palm that clearly received plenty of tender loving care.

Caroline was curious. Why hadn't Sir Arthur mentioned that there was another woman member in Chambers? Why hadn't Matt. . .? Well, it didn't matter, she told herself briskly—it would be nice not to be the only one. She sat down at the desk that had been Bill Latimer's, and smoothed her hand over the well-worn leather top, a small smile curving her mouth. It was good to be back.

CHAPTER EIGHT

THE Reckless Driving brief was fairly straight-forward—it should ease her back into practice nicely. She was getting quite absorbed in it when the sound of light footsteps on the stairs brought her head up. The door opened, and her new co-tenant breezed in.

Caroline found herself the subject of a high-nosed stare. 'You must be Caroline.' A beautifully manicured hand was extended in a gesture that was faintly condescending. 'How do you do? I'm Harriet Pearson—dreadful name, isn't it? I've never quite forgiven the wrinklies for saddling me with it. Call me Harry.'

The words were friendly enough, but they were spoken in a crisp, indifferent manner that robbed them of any sincerity. Caroline felt a shadow of disappointment—but, after all, it was a little pre-mature to assume that she was going to dislike the girl. She returned her a pleasant smile as she shook her hand. 'Hello.'

'I see you've taken Bill's desk,' Harry went on, barely acknowledging her response. 'You didn't want your old one back, did you? Only it would be such a drag to move everything around. And I am rather busy—I'm on a Murder with Sir Arthur. I've just finished my pupillage with him. He's super, isn't he? So distinguished.'

Caroline slanted her a look of astonishment. Sir

Arthur was a nice old stick, but he hardly warranted that kind of husky-voiced admiration. And she would never have thought he could be lured from the straight path to his silver wedding anniversary by a girl younger than his own daughter— even one as undeniably attractive as Harriet Pearson.

Now, if she had spoken of Matt in those tones, she would have understood it. She was rather Matt's type. Thick, shiny ash-blonde hair that swung in a straight bob to her shoulders, and legs like a racehorse. And an air of cool self-possession that most women didn't acquire until they were in their thirties.

'Sir Arthur's a very good teacher,' she agreed, trying to make conversation.

'Excellent. Of course, he's related to my mother—some kind of second cousin. . .'

Caroline glanced at her in surprise as her voice trailed away, and then turned to the door. Matt had appeared. Suddenly the atmosphere in the room fairly crackled with electric tension. Harry had picked up some papers, and was shuffling them around busily, her eyes evasive.

Matt ignored the girl's presence—a little too pointedly. 'Want to come down and have a look at this Third Party Negligence?' he asked Caroline.

'Now? Oh. . .yes, of course. I'd be glad to,' she agreed quickly, picking up her notebook and pen. He stood aside to let her precede him through the door—it took a lot of will-power not to look back and see what Harry's reaction was. At least now she knew—that apparent interest in Sir Arthur had been as phoney as she had thought it. Harriet Pearson *was* Matt's type.

What had been going on while she had been away? Of course, she couldn't expect that there hadn't been other women, but it had come as rather a shock to be faced with the evidence so soon. And what was going on now? Was the affair over? Or was it continuing in secret? After all, the only reason he had proposed to her was to give Vicky a father—she could hardly demand that he be faithful.

It was fortunate that she had found out the truth at once—it would make it a little easier to control the temptation to yield to his persuasion. But common sense couldn't ease the ache in her heart.

Matt followed her down the stairs to his office— it was one of the biggest in the building, with a fine chandelier and a lovely old mahogany partners' desk. The walls were lined to the ceiling with books and boxes of files, and the slightly uneven floor was covered with a square of red and gold carpet, old but still glowing with rich colour.

'Have a seat,' he invited pleasantly. 'No, not there,' he urged as she moved to one of the clients' chairs beside the desk. 'We might as well be comfortable.' He indicated one of the deep armchairs on the other side of the room.

Caroline sat down, crossing her legs and assuming her coolest professional manner. It wasn't going to be easy, but she could at least make sure that she put everything on a completely businesslike footing from the very beginning. Fortunately Matt seemed to share that intention.

'I'm glad you've agreed to give me a hand with

this one,' he said, his tone as bland as if there had never been any more between them than a few academic tussles in court. 'I think it raises some interesting points of law.'

Two hours later she knew exactly why everyone said Matthew Farrar-Reid was brilliant. He had a memory like a computer, and a very shrewd ability to get straight to the heart of a problem. He sat back in his own armchair, apparently totally at his ease, and dissected the whole case, picking out every salient point.

'Well, I think that wraps it up for now,' he said at last. 'If you could begin drafting a reply, and let me have it as soon as possible?'

She nodded, pleased that he had entrusted her with the task. 'I'll have it for you tomorrow.'

He smiled, and her heart missed half a beat. 'Don't burn the midnight oil too long over it,' he advised.

'Oh, I'm enjoying being back at the grindstone so much, I don't mind,' she returned with a light laugh. 'Not that Vicky's likely to let me concentrate for long!' Suddenly she felt uncomfortable—the mention of Vicky's name seemed out of place here. 'Well, I. . .I'll be seeing you,' she flustered, picking up her pen and pad. 'I want to spend a couple of hours reading up the Road Traffic Acts this afternoon—I'm afraid I've got rather rusty.'

She escaped quickly, hurrying up the stairs to her own room. Harry was still in court, fortunately—she probably wouldn't be back for lunch. That was a relief—Caroline needed a little time to think over what she had observed this morning, and in the meantime it was easier if she didn't have to put up a façade of friendliness.

She was going to have to be careful—once before she had let jealousy of another woman goad her into a fatal mistake. And Harriet Pearson was far more formidable as a rival than Anthea had been.

Life settled very quickly into its new routine. There were really only two problems. The first was with Lisle, the au pair. The girl just didn't seem to be settling down. She spoke little English, though almost certainly more than she pretended to, and she was so slow that it was all Caroline could do to keep her temper with her.

Then one afternoon Caroline came home from work to find the girl curled up in an armchair with a box of chocolates, while Vicky was crying with wet pants. When the same thing happened a week later she blew her top. The girl collapsed in floods of tears, but Caroline was too angry to feel sorry for her. Two hours later her bags were packed and she was on her way to Victoria Station to catch a train for Gatwick Airport.

It was a worry, having to get another girl—she even began to wonder if she was wise to do so. Maybe Matt had been right all along, and she should not consider working until Vicky was a little older. But she would give it one more chance.

Fortunately, the agency were very good, and sent another girl within two days—a pretty, vivacious Swiss girl called Tina. She couldn't have been more unlike Lisle: quick, willing—and she could cook too. Vicky took to her at once, which was an enormous relief.

The second problem didn't seem to offer such an easy prospect of solution. As every day passed Caroline's conviction grew that something was going on between Matt and Harry. It was in the way they avoided each other, pretended not to notice when the other was in the room.

It would have been natural, surely, when she was working with Matt, for him to ask how she was getting along with her new co-tenant, or for Harry to speculate—as everyone else did—whether Matt was going to apply to take silk this year? But neither of them so much as mentioned the other's name.

She was finding it increasingly difficult to handle the emotional turmoil the situation was generating. She was working with Matt quite closely, and every weekend he would come over to visit Vicky. But he seemed to have no difficulty in separating everything into neatly labelled compartments.

She envied him his sang-froid even as it infuriated her. It was hard to know what he was thinking—although he paid her a few light compliments on her appearance he didn't try to overstep the boundary that she had drawn in their relationship, nor did he raise the subject of marriage again. But she sensed that he hadn't given up—he wasn't the type.

By mid-May the weather had turned beautifully warm, every day bright and sunny. The Saturday before the Bank Holiday they decided to take Vicky to the zoo. The little girl loved it—Matt sat her on his shoulders, and she squealed with delight at this lofty vantage-point from which she could see everything.

They showed her the pandas and the cockatoos, the penguins and the sea-lions, and bought ice-creams that melted on their chins as they stood watching the great prowling bears. It was almost as if they were a real family.

With a jolt of alarm, Caroline realised how dangerously she had been wavering in her resolve. It was a trap that would be all too easy to slide into. Was that his intention? The subtle approach, sneaking past her guard, making her come to depend on him without her even realising it?

He had been succeeding, almost impercepti-bly—over the past couple of months she had really begun to like him. He could be an amusing companion, and a sympathetic listener when she was under stress at work, or worried about Vicky.

And always there was that disturbing element of physical attraction, all the time she was aware of the hard, muscular maleness of his body. Today he was wearing cream-coloured American chinos and a light sweater, and already the sun had streaked his hair with blond. She had made love with this man, she had felt his strong arms around her, breathed the subtle musky fragrance of his skin. . .

Suddenly he glanced round, and caught her watching him. She turned away quickly, her heart racing. 'What would you like to do now?' he asked, his voice a little too bland. 'Shall we go through and have a look at the camels and giraffes?'

'If you like,' she responded with difficulty.

There was a glint of mocking amusement in his eyes, as if he had been able to read her mind. Caroline hurried down the steps of the terrace, and led the way through the tunnel under the main road, that led to the northern half of the zoo.

She could hear his footsteps behind her, and she could feel him watching her. Had it been a mistake to wear these jeans? They were a little tight, moulding the slim shape of her body rather intimately. It hadn't seemed to matter this morning, when she was getting dressed, but now. . .She didn't want Matt looking at her like that.

She was on edge for the rest of the afternoon, conscious of a subtle shift in the atmosphere between them. The truce was over. It was her own fault—she had let him glimpse a chink in her armour, even if only for that fleeting moment, and thereby had awakened an old danger.

It was just the same as before—while she could maintain that hard outer shell, she had been safe. But as soon as he had found out that there was a softness within, he had wanted to reach out and take it. It was an added jeopardy—what a sweetener for swallowing the pill of responsibility for his child, to have the prospect of warming his nights with a wife who couldn't quite resist his advances.

By the time they got back to the flat it was Vicky's teatime. 'What would you like to eat, darling?' Caroline asked as Matt carried her into the kitchen.

She gave the matter grave consideration, and then announced triumphantly, 'Want. . .cake!'

Caroline laughed. 'You can't have just cake for tea,' she protested.

'Why not?' teased Matt, bouncing the little girl in his arms. He set her down on a chair at the kitchen-table, and crouched down beside her. 'Cake's nice.'

'You're spoiling her,' she accused him mildly.

'Why shouldn't I?' he countered, a rough edge creeping into his voice. 'I have little enough chance to be with her.'

Caroline was instantly on the defensive. 'You see her every weekend.'

'Oh, big deal. That's not what I want, and you know it.' He moved towards her, and she retreated instinctively around the table. 'Let's put an end to this nonsense, Caro. We can get married quietly. . .'

'No! Don't start that again,' she snapped. 'I've told you, I'm not going to marry you.' She glared at him, breathless from the rapid beat of her heart. She was on a knife-edge—it would be so easy to give in, do what he wanted. Vicky sensed the sudden spark of tension between them. She stared from one to the other in bewilderment, and her little face puckered with tears. Caroline snatched her up into her arms, hugging her close. 'You're upsetting her,' she threw at him fiercely.

'*I'm* upsetting her? If you weren't so damned selfish and obstinate. . .'

Her eyes flashed. '*I'm* obstinate?'

Matt seemed to be having difficulty leashing his anger. 'Don't you think you're being a little unfair on Vicky?' he asked.

'Not at all.'

'Damn you!' He struck the frame of the door with his fist. 'There's no talking any sense to you.'

'I believe I'm talking perfect sense,' she retorted evenly. 'Now, I think you'd better go.' She reached for a piece of kitchen towel and dabbed Vicky's tears away. 'Say goodnight to Daddy, sweetheart.'

He glared at her, silently accusing her of using the child as a defence—a charge to which she could only plead guilty. 'Very well,' he conceded through clenched teeth. 'We'll talk about it another time.'

'There's nothing further to discuss,' she stated flatly. 'There's no point in our getting married, it's as simple as that.'

His mouth thinned with impatience, but he let the subject drop. He took Vicky and gave her a big hug and a kiss. 'You are still bringing her down to Suffolk next weekend?' he asked.

She would have liked to refuse, but she really couldn't. 'Of course,' she confirmed reluctantly.

'Good.' He gave the child back to her, and with a grim nod of farewell left the flat.

'Dad-dad!' protested Vicky, trying to wriggle out of Caroline's arms.

Caroline caught her close, feeling herself on the edge of tears. 'No, sweetheart. Daddy's gone now, but you'll see him next weekend,' she promised. 'Now, sit down at the table like a good girl, and Mummy will get you some tea—and some cake. Would you like that?'

The little girl hesitated, but the offer was enough to distract her. 'Yes,' she lisped, nodding her head emphatically.

'Come along, then. Let's see, what shall we

have? How about. . .a nice omelette, with mush-rooms in?'

A quarter of an hour later they were sitting at the kitchen-table, talking about all the animals they had seen, as they ate their tea. Caroline was always fascinated by how quickly her child was developing and learning things; there seemed to be something new every day—new words she was learning and stringing together into sentences, new skills like learning to put her own shoes on.

That was something she was denying Matt, the chance to enjoy these everyday little triumphs. And was it fair on Vicky? She had asked herself that question a thousand times. The child adored him—there were always tears when it was time for him to leave. *Was* she being selfish?

The doubts were still lingering in her brain when the telephone rang. Vicky jumped down from the table, and ran over to pick it up—she knew exactly who it was that always called after tea on a Saturday.

'Nanna? H'lo. We been zoo,' she gabbled excit-edly. She listened to her grandmother's voice at the other end of the transatlantic line, her eyes wide with delight.

Caroline went over and knelt beside her, sharing the receiver. 'Did you see the elephants?' Betty was asking.

Vicky nodded solemnly. 'They was this big!' she described, holding her hand up as high as she could reach.

Caroline laughed, taking the phone and settling the child on her knees, where she began weaving her fingers into the coil of the wire. 'Mum? Hi, how are you? And how's Check?'

'Oh, we're just great. And business is booming.' Her mother, much to her surprise, had opened a dance studio which she was running extremely successfully. 'We're thinking of opening another floor and putting in a multi-gym. This fitness trend is showing no sign of slowing down, thank goodness. Vicky sounds well—she was telling me you've been to the zoo today.'

'Yes—with Matt.'

'Hmm. And how are things with him?'

'Oh, much the same,' Caroline responded in a wry tone. 'We're going down to Suffolk next weekend, to see his family.'

'Oh?'

'Just so his father can meet Vicky. I promised.'

'You sound as if you're not too keen to go. Don't let him put any pressure on you, darling. There's no reason why you should do anything you don't want to do. Thirty years ago it was different, but today you can stand up for your rights.'

Caroline smiled to herself. She could never have imagined having a discussion like this with her mother before—but Betty had changed in many ways, far beyond the crisp New York accent she had acquired. The difference was that she felt herself to be loved. Check adored his mature, confident lady, and it had transformed her life.

'Don't worry about me, Mum—I can take care of myself,' she promised. 'By the way, have you heard from Dad lately?'

'I had a letter last week. Erina's pregnant again.'

'Already? It's only a couple of months since she had the last one.'

Betty laughed drily. 'She's got him firmly tied to hearth and home. Between keeping her temper sweet, and the shooting schedule he's on, he's got neither the time nor the energy to mess around. It could be the making of him.'

'No regrets, Mum?'

'Are you kidding? I wish I'd made the break years ago. Too scared, I guess. Don't you make the same mistake, honey. There's happiness out there somewhere, if you've just got the guts to find it.'

'Right,' agreed Caroline. 'Well, cheerio, Mum—I'll ring you next week.'

'Cheers, honey—and don't forget you promised to come over in the summer—I want to see my granddaughter again.'

'Of course. Bye, Mum.'

She put the phone down, and regarded it pensively for a moment. Her mother's advice was timely, reminding her of the original reasons for her refusal to marry Matt. It would be different if he had been in love with her, but he wasn't. And if she married him she would be repeating her parents' mistake, and she had always vowed she would never inflict that on a child of hers.

Oh, he wouldn't treat her as Adam had treated Betty, he wouldn't flaunt his affairs at her or neglect her for months on end—he was too much of a gentleman for that. But he would know that she was in love with him—married to him, sharing his bed, she would never be able to hide it.

Love—that dangerous emotion whose very

existence she had once tried to deny. If she married Matt, every day would be an aching misery. Because, however courteous and considerate he was towards her, he would never love her as she loved him.

Caroline was in court for most of the following week, at the Old Bailey. It was gratifying how quickly she had been able to pick up the threads of her career again. A barrister's reputation, like an actor's, was only as good as their last performance. But Hugh had done some good work on her behalf, and instructing solicitors were beginning to ask for her by name again, and sending her some very interesting briefs.

She saw little of Matt except for a few brief encounters in Hugh's office, always with several other people around. But on Friday afternoon, as she was coming out of Court Seven, where her case was being heard, she saw him. He was half hidden by one of the large rectangular columns that supported the ceiling, and he was leaning close to someone, engaged in what was clearly a very intense conversation. And that someone, she wouldn't mind betting, was Harriet Pearson.

She turned aside and walked quickly towards the lifts, her heels tapping a brisk tattoo on the hard grey floor. There weren't many people about—her case had finished later than usual. She pressed the button to summon one of the lifts, and stood waiting for it to arrive, tempted almost beyond endurance to glance over her shoulder to check whether her surmise had been correct.

Not till the steel doors were actually opening did

she succumb, just briefly. She had been right—
there was no mistaking that elegant profile and
thick ash-blonde hair. As if he sensed her gaze,
Matt looked up suddenly, catching her eye. She
turned away quickly, and stepped into the lift.

Behind her she heard hurrying footsteps, and at
the very last moment as the lift doors were closing
Matt stepped through them. 'Caro! I'm glad I
caught you,' he said, smiling down at her as if
there were nothing wrong between them at all.
'We haven't sorted out the arrangements for the
weekend yet.'

'Oh. . .yes. The weekend. Actually, Matt,
I. . .I'm not sure if I can come. I'm in the middle
of a case, and I need to go over the papers again. I
start my defence on Tuesday.'

'You shouldn't spend the whole weekend on it,'
Matt advised, with the wisdom of a past-master.
'I'm sure you've prepared it as fully as you can. If
you spend too much time going over it now, you'll
get stale. Come away for the weekend, and forget
all about it. Leave it till Monday afternoon, and
then give it a read through.'

'I don't know. . .'

'You look tired,' he said with a sympathy that
undermined her will. 'Why don't you go home
and get an early night? I'll pick you up in the
morning, about ten.'

'All right.' She *was* tired—too tired to argue. The
lift had reached the ground floor, and she stepped
out. 'See you tomorrow.' She managed a fleeting
smile of farewell, nodded an acknowledgement to
the police guard in the vestibule as he called out a
cheerful, 'Goodnight, Miss Kosek,' and pushed

through the revolving door, not waiting to see if Matt was following her.

It must have been a lovely day outside the cool environs of the Central Criminal Court—the Tube was packed with cheerful people, going home from work in shirtsleeves, looking forward to the long weekend. Caroline had to stand all the way to Earl's Court, holding on to a strap as the train jolted and swayed.

She should have been more insistent in refusing to go with Matt this weekend. But it really wasn't fair to his father to cancel the visit at the last minute—Matt had told her several times how much he was looking forward to seeing his granddaughter.

But, after this, she was going to make a few changes to the arrangements. There was no longer any need for her to be around when he came—she could arrange that Tina would hand Vicky over and collect her. Maybe she would even think about moving to another set of Chambers. It would be much easier if she didn't have to see so much of him.

Matt was on time, as always. And in spite of her reservations it was a pleasant drive out to Suffolk. Vicky slept contentedly all the way, and it seemed that Matt had decided to ignore—for now, at least—the subject of their last argument.

It was a beautiful day. The spring sunshine filtered down through the young green leaves of the oak trees that lined the road, and sparkled on the lazy river that flowed alongside. 'Oh! It's lovely,' sighed Caroline, drinking in the scenery.

He quirked an enquiring eyebrow. 'Better than California?'

'Well, different,' she mused. 'Everything's more. . .flamboyant there, more melodramatic. Nothing seems to be done by halves.'

He laughed, but there was a sharp glint in his eyes as he glanced towards her. 'You know, you never told me why you decided to come back,' he said. 'Was there a row with some boyfriend?'

She hesitated, resenting the probing question. 'No, there wasn't,' she responded coolly.

'No row, or no boyfriend?'

'There were one or two,' she countered, hostility lending an edge to her voice. 'Not that it's any of your business. I haven't asked you about. . .about the girlfriends you've had.'

'But then I haven't had custody of Vicky,' he pointed out, a cold light glittering in those blue eyes.

'What's that got to do with anything?'

'Don't you think I have a right to know if you have any serious plans?'

Caroline quickly hid her surprise at his words. Serious plans? There hadn't even been any boy-friends—though she wasn't going to tell him that. 'I don't anticipate that I'll be making any serious plans just yet,' she informed him coolly. 'But if I do, I'll let you know.'

He accepted that concession with a terse nod, and they drove for a while in silence. Caroline watched him covertly, her thoughts in a tangle. She had been looking forward to this trip, to meeting Matt's family, with a certain amount of trepidation. What were they going to think of her, having an illegitimate child?

And since last weekend, when it had become apparent that he hadn't given up the idea of marrying her, her anxiety had increased. He had found that the oblique approach, trying to engage her in a friendly relationship until marriage seemed a natural step, wasn't going to work. Would he now try coercion? She shivered. Matt Farrar-Reid was a man accustomed to getting his own way—and she knew to her cost how dangerous he could be.

It was almost lunchtime when they turned off the main road. After a short drive along narrower country lanes they came to a small village, and just beyond it Matt turned the car through a five-bar red gate in a low stone wall, and drew up before a long two-storey house covered with ivy.

She wasn't sure what she had been expecting—apprehension had painted a picture of an imposing stately home. This was a farmhouse, albeit a large one, built of the local grey flint which glinted in the sun as if set with filaments of dark glass. Beside it was a large duck-pond, set amid willow trees, reflecting the pure blue of the sky.

As Caroline looked around, admiring the perfect tranquillity of the scene, the front door burst open, and a tribe of small boys erupted around them. 'Hey, Uncle Matt, what a *super* car! How fast does it go? Has it got an overhead camshaft?' they demanded excitedly, swarming all over the vehicle.

'Hey, keep your mucky fingermarks off it!' he

ordered them cheerfully. 'And where are your manners? Say hello to Caroline.'

The boys stood back for a moment, smiling sheepishly. 'Oh. . .hello,' they conceded, but their interest was all for the car. 'What sort of engine has it got? Will you open the bonnet and let us look?'

'Later,' he insisted, shepherding them all towards the house. 'These are my cousins' children,' he added to Caroline. 'This is John, that one's Mark. . .Oh, you'll get the hang of their names as you go along.'

'Yes, I. . .expect so,' she murmured faintly. 'How many of them are there?'

'Well, there's my Aunt Lilian, and my cousin Sara with her brood—she lost her husband a couple of years ago. Then there's my other cousin Tom and his family—he runs a farm over by Wickham Market. And his brother Michael's here with his lot—two boys and two girls—they always come down for the Bank Holiday.'

'Oh.' She turned away to lift Vicky out of the back of the car. He had warned her that his family would be there—but she hadn't been expecting that there would be so many of them. It was going to be even worse than she had expected.

CHAPTER NINE

IT SEEMED that all the family had come out to greet them. Caroline managed some sort of smile, wishing the earth would open up and swallow her. There seemed to be dozens of them. Matt put his hand on her arm and drew her forward.

'Come and meet my father,' he urged quietly.

She would have needed no introduction to Sir Lionel Farrar-Reid; he had all the commanding presence of his son, that same hard-boned, clever face, those same steel-blue eyes—still shrewdly intelligent, though he was well into his seventies and walked with the aid of an ebony cane.

'Good afternoon, my dear,' he greeted her with formal courtesy, offering her his hand. Caroline shook it, murmuring something polite, and he turned to the child in her arms, his expression softening. 'Well, so you're my granddaughter,' he mused. 'You're a proper little Farrar-Reid too, aren't you?'

Vicky responded at once to the warmth in his voice, and held out her chubby little arms to him. He took her, cuddling her close, and Caroline could have sworn that it was a tear she saw sparkling in the corner of his eye. He turned to her, and smiled. 'Thank you for bringing her,' he said simply.

She couldn't answer—there was a great big lump in her throat. All she could manage was a wavering smile in response, and a nod of her head. She was glad that Vicky was the centre of attention—it gave her a few minutes to gather her composure.

One of the women came towards her with a welcoming smile. 'Hello, Caroline,' she greeted her pleasantly. 'I'm Sara. Do come in. I'm sorry you're having us all thrust upon you at once, but you'll soon get used to us. Let me make the introductions. These two scruffy brats are mine.' She cuffed two of the boys affectionately round the head. 'The big one's called Mark, and the other one's David. And this is my mother.'

Aunt Lilian was quite as formidable as her brother, but she too had a smile of considerable charm. 'How do you do, my dear. I'm very pleased to meet you. Did you have a pleasant drive?'

Caroline took the slim hand that was held out to her. 'Yes, thank you,' she smiled in response. 'I've never been to Suffolk before—it's such a beautiful county.'

Aunt Lilian laughed. 'In this season, yes—but I'm afraid in winter it can be quite a different story! Now, I'm sure you'll want to freshen up before lunch. Matthew, take Caroline up and show her to her room.'

Matt's lips twitched with appreciative humour at the imperiousness of the command, but he replied mildly, 'Of course.'

Caroline hesitated, glancing uncertainly towards Vicky. The older woman smiled understandingly. 'I think she'll be all right for a few minutes,' she assured her. 'We'll look after her.'

'Of course—thank you.' There was a trace of

reluctance in her concession. It seemed as though Vicky had been taken over, taken from her. It was foolish to resent that, of course. She had the child with her all the time—they had only this one weekend.

She followed Matt into the house, looking around her with interest. It was a big house, a warren of stairways and corridors. All the floors gleamed with well-polished parquet, scattered with rugs of good quality, but there were fishing-rods in the hall, and children's bicycles under the stairs. Although the atmosphere breathed discreet wealth, the house had a lived-in feel about it too. It was a family home, not a showpiece.

She was definitely beginning to regret that she had come. Matt's family had been a shadowy entity, easily discounted. Now that was no longer possible—that moment of meeting between Vicky and her grandfather would not be easily forgotten.

Matt turned a corner of the corridor, and opened a door on a large, comfortable bedroom, furnished in restful shades of lavender blue. The furniture, like the house, was substantial, but not too ornate. And there was a big double bed, which she regarded with a certain amount of misgiving.

Matt caught her eye with a gleam of sardonic humour. 'Don't worry—I won't be sharing it with you,' he told her drily. 'My room's opposite.'

She chose to ignore that attempt to needle her. 'Thank you,' she said coolly. 'I'll see you at lunch.'

'Will you be able to find your way back downstairs?'

'I think so.'

'Then I'll leave you.' He went out, closing the door behind him.

Caroline sat down on the edge of the bed, and drew a deep breath, trying to still the turmoil in her mind. She was angry with Matt for bringing her here—she felt as if he was trying some kind of emotional blackmail on her, to make her feel guilty for keeping Vicky away from this side of her family.

Well, she wasn't going to let it work, she vowed resolutely. She had made up her mind that she wasn't going to marry him, and she was going to stick to that decision—no matter what tricks he used.

Caroline had just finished changing from the slacks she had travelled down in to a cool white linen dress, when there was a tap on the door. She called, 'Come in,' and Matt's cousin Sara opened the door, Vicky in her arms. 'Oh, hello,' she smiled, hurrying over to take the child. 'Has she been good?'

'She's been golden,' Sara assured her, buffing the little girl's rosy cheek. 'We just came to find you because I thought you might have trouble finding your way back downstairs—I'm afraid this place is a bit of a rabbit warren!'

'It's a beautiful house,' Caroline commented as she carried Vicky into the bathroom to wash her face and hands before lunch. 'How old is it?'

'Oh, hundreds of years. Well, the parish records mention it as far back as 1533. You can still see the timber framing in the north wing, though it's all been covered over with brick. It's a dreadful place to keep clean, though.'

'I bet it is,' agreed Caroline sympathetically. 'Do you have help?'

'Oh, don't talk to me about help!' sighed Sara, rolling her eyes expressively. 'Mrs Lacey's a blessing, but she only does the cooking now, and the trouble I've had, finding someone reliable to come in and do the cleaning!'

'Really? I'd have thought it would be easier out here in the country—there aren't many other jobs available.'

'Don't you believe it. The youngsters don't want to go into service these days—they'd rather travel miles into town and work in a factory.'

Caroline smiled. She rather liked Sara, she decided. About the same age as herself, she had an open, friendly face, and a manner that was entirely lacking in affectation. 'I know the problem,' she confided. 'I've had the same trouble getting someone to look after Vicky. I've got an au pair at the moment, and she's very good, but she'll only be staying for a year. It isn't really satisfactory.'

'Well, you should make Matt do something about it,' Sara advised her briskly. 'He's got to take on his share of the responsibility. Actually, you know, I think it would do him good,' she added confidentially. 'He's never taken life very seriously—everything's always come too easily to him. That's why he wouldn't go into the Bank with Uncle Leo—and I'm sure he took up climbing for the same reason. He needs the challenge. But a family of his own would give him some sort of centre to his life.'

Caroline shook her head. 'Oh, I don't see us becoming a family,' she demurred.

'Why not?' argued Sara, rushing in well-intentioned. 'Anyone can see that he adores Vicky. And the fact that he's brought you down here to meet his family. . .Well, I wouldn't be surprised if he's thinking seriously of getting married.'

Caroline bit her lip—what could she possibly say to that? Maybe it was best to be honest right from the start. 'As a matter of fact,' she confessed diffidently, 'he's already asked me. And I said no.'

'Oh.' Sara looked embarrassed. 'I'm sorry—my big mouth! It's none of my business, of course. But it's a shame—I'd love to see him happily settled down. He's always been my favourite cousin. And I've always felt he was. . .lonely, somehow—his mother dying when he was so young, and having no brothers and sisters of his own. And he and Uncle Leo haven't always got on—they're a bit too much alike. And Uncle Leo will be disappointed—he's really taken to little Vicky, and I'm sure he wishes she were truly a part of the family. Still, it isn't really any of my business,' she added with a wry shrug. 'Are you ready to go down to lunch now?'

'Oh . . .yes, just give me a minute to brush Vicky's hair.'

There was a pleasant informality about the Farrar-Reid household that came as a surprise to Caroline. The children—though far from being spoiled—were very much at the centre of things.

And Vicky had clearly made an instant hit with everyone.

After lunch, they all adjourned to the garden to play a scratch game of cricket—the whole family joined in, the rules being adapted to suit the needs of young and old. To Caroline, who had grown up as an only child in a household dominated by her father's whims and moods, it was a revelation.

She was sitting out, waiting for her turn to bat again, watching as Matt helped Vicky take her stroke, when Sir Lionel came over and sat down beside her. She managed a smile, feeling acutely aware of the awkwardness of the situation.

'She's a delightful child,' he remarked.

'Thank you.'

'I hope you won't mind my saying so,' he went on in a quiet voice, 'but I make no secret of it that I was very disappointed that you decided against marrying my son. I think you would have been very good for him. And he takes his responsibilities towards the little one very seriously, you know.'

It wasn't easy to answer. 'I. . .I'm sorry,' she managed to say. 'It just wouldn't have worked out.'

He smiled. 'I can understand your wariness. I'm afraid he hasn't earned himself the best sort of reputation in some respects.' He glanced towards Matthew, who was chasing one of the spaniels who had run off with the cricket ball. 'But I feel sure that you could change that—a woman of your intelligence.'

Caroline sought in vain for the words to make him understand. But fortunately at that moment Aunt Lilian—who was acting as scorekeeper and referee—announced that it was time for tea. Mrs Lacey had brought a tray out on to the terrace, and the children and dogs quickly forgot their game in their eagerness to scamper over and claim a slice of home-made fruitcake.

'Now sit down properly,' Aunt Lilian scolded sternly. 'Everyone will get some if they take their turn. Mark, you may help me pour. Caroline, would Vicky like milk and a dash, or shall I send one of the children to get her some squash?'

'Oh—no, thank you. She likes tea,' Caroline assured her quickly. 'What do you say?' she added to the child as Aunt Lilian handed her a half-filled cup.

'T'ank you,' the little girl responded obediently, turning on one of her winning smiles.

'That's a good girl,' approved the elderly woman warmly. 'She's a credit to you, my dear.'

Caroline smiled with gratified pride. 'Thank you.'

'I dare say I'm an interfering old busybody,' Aunt Lilian went on in the same brisk tone, 'but I do trust that the two of you will do the right thing by the child now. It may be acceptable to your generation, this arrangement of yours, but it isn't acceptable to mine—and I wonder if it will be acceptable to her in the future.'

Caroline felt her cheeks flame scarlet, and mumbled something incoherent. She really couldn't blame Matt's family for expressing their opinions—she had known what it would be like when she had agreed to come. It was fortunate that they were only staying for a few days—she didn't think she could face any more than that.

*   *   *

In the midst of all his lively family, Caroline had few moments alone with Matt. It wasn't until after dinner, when they had all returned to the drawing-room, that he came over and sat down beside her. 'You seemed to be getting along very well with my father,' he remarked quietly.

She slanted him a brittle smile. 'Oh, yes—they're all very nice. Except they're all trying to persuade me to marry you,' she informed him drily.

He laughed. 'Poor Caro,' he taunted. 'Feeling besieged?'

'Nothing I can't handle,' she returned, managing to sound quite cool. 'I was besieged by one of the best—my mother—for years. I've never thought marriage had a great deal to recommend it.'

'Don't you think that depends largely on the parties involved?'

'Quite possibly,' she conceded. 'But I don't think there's any reason to suppose that you and I could make a success of it.'

'Don't you? I can think of one *very* good reason.'

The look he gave her made her blood run hot. She was furious with him for embarrassing her like this in front of his family—not that they could have overheard his words, but she was sure they must have noticed the effect they had on her. She stood up quickly. 'I. . .excuse me, I'd better go and look in on Vicky,' she mumbled, and made a hasty escape.

So that was to be his next move—she had been afraid of that all along. Her mouth felt suddenly dry. Though he hadn't touched her since she had returned from America, she knew herself to be all too vulnerable.

Vicky was fast asleep in her cot, her long silky lashes shadowing her rosy round cheeks. Caroline leaned over her, gazing down at her with loving eyes. She was such a little darling when she was asleep.

'Everything OK?'

She glanced up sharply as Matt whispered from the door. He tiptoed across the room and looked down into the cot, his expression softening into a smile. He put out one strong, gentle hand and lifted the coverlet protectively over the little girl's shoulder, careful not to disturb her slumbers.

Caroline drew back, finding his proximity a little unnerving. She crept softly from the room, and he followed her, closing the door quietly behind him. In the subdued glow of light from the stairs she could see his face, but not his eyes, and a prickle of nervous apprehension scudded down her spine. As she tried to move away, he caught her hand and drew her inexorably against him, his arm encircling her waist.

'Well, Miss Kosek, what do we do now?' he taunted, a strangely enigmatic smile curving that arrogant, sensual mouth.

Caroline felt her breath warm on her lips as she stared up at him. 'Wh. . .what do you mean?' she stammered.

'You know what I mean,' he murmured, his voice taking on a husky timbre. 'How do we break the stalemate? You won't marry me, and I don't seem able to persuade you. . .' A glint of speculation lurked in the depths of his eyes. 'Unless. . .'

He bent his head, his mouth brushing hers, lightly, tantalisingly, and the tip of his tongue probed the sensitive corners of her lips. A tremor of shock ran through her, and she tried to pull away from him, but he held her prisoner.

'Not so fast,' he chided, his warm breath fanning her cheek. 'I'm trying a little experiment.'

She held herself rigid as the sensuous tip of his tongue swirled around the delicate shell of her ear, and his teeth nipped gently at her lobe. A wave of heat swept through her veins, but still she struggled to defend herself against his expert technique.

He laughed softly, as if he found her resistance amusing. And slowly, inevitably, he was winning. The warm male muskiness of his body was drugging her senses, reminding her all too vividly of that fateful night in Cannes. The steel in her spine was slowly melting as he moulded her intimately close against him.

He had remembered that there was an exquisitely sensitive spot in the hollow of her shoulder, and had found it unerringly, his mouth hot against her skin. An odd little moan purred from her throat, and her head tipped back as her heartbeat raced dizzyingly out of control.

This time when his lips closed over hers he found a helpless surrender. With unhurried ease he sought the inner softness of her mouth, a deliberately flagrant exploration that rekindled the long-slumbering embers of desire deep inside her.

A languid warmth was spreading through her body, as sensual longings flamed under the expert persuasion of his kiss. His caressing touch was playing havoc with her senses, consuming her ability to think. She was aware only of the shaming urgency of her own need, and knew that every tremor of her body must betray her weakness to him.

She felt his hand wandering to the soft swell of her breast, and her breath stopped in her throat. She was clinging to him, desperately seeking some solid support in a world that was floating, a world in which time had no meaning and reason no place.

What would have happened she dared not imagine, but abruptly the dark spell was shattered by the sound of a footfall at the other end of the corridor. 'Oh. . .' Sara laughed uncertainly. 'I'm sorry. . .I didn't realise. . .the two of you were up here,' she explained.

Caroline tore herself out of Matt's arms, her heart thudding so hard that it was painful even to breathe. 'Oh. . .I was just coming down again,' she managed to say. 'I. . .I just popped up to see that Vicky was all right.'

'Of course.' The hint of satisfaction in her voice told Caroline that Matt's cousin was convinced she had stumbled on a romantic secret tryst.

It was a relief when the weekend was over. The glorious weather had broken, and the rain was falling steadily on Tuesday when Caroline returned to work. She stood at the window, watching the droplets hit the glass and slide slowly down, running together.

What was she going to do? If she were simply to enumerate the pros and cons, she had to admit that there were several good reasons for marrying

Matt. Not least of them was his family. She really like them—especially Sara, who she would have chosen for a friend. And now that her parents were divorced, and apparently settled in the most distant corners of the globe, it would be nice for Vicky to be part of such a happy family.

And Vicky was so fond of him. . .Oh, dammit, she was letting her emotions twist her round in circles, when what she needed to do above all was think clearly. It was becoming increasingly apparent that Matt was not going to give up easily. He was accustomed to getting his own way, and it seemed he was prepared to use the most unscrupulous means to get it. A shimmer of heat ran through her as her body vividly recalled the way he had kissed her.

Maybe she could try discussing the problem rationally with him. Perhaps they could come to some arrangement. Oh, that was stupid, she chided herself crossly. With Matt Farrar-Reid, it would be all or nothing. All. . .Dreams and images swirled in her brain, heating her blood.

She turned sharply as the door behind her opened. Harry breezed into the room and dumped her crocodile-skin briefcase on her desk. 'Hi,' she greeted Caroline casually. 'Have a nice weekend?'

'Yes, thank you.' Caroline had wondered how Harry was going to behave towards her—she had been sure that Matt had been telling her about their plans when she had seen the two of them together in court on Friday. But Harry seemed unconcerned. Suddenly Caroline couldn't take the play-acting any longer. 'As a matter of fact,' she announced baldly, 'I went down to Suffolk—with Matt.'

Only by the briefest hesitation did the elegant blonde betray that her cool composure had been disturbed. 'Lord—how dull!' she drawled in a tone of supreme boredom. 'How could you stand it? It's miles from anywhere—and all those awful fossilised relatives of his!'

It was Caroline's turn to hide her reaction. So Matt had taken Harry down to Suffolk! Their affair really must have been serious. She forced herself to respond in an airy tone, 'As a matter of fact I enjoyed it—such a pretty place.'

'I dare say,' conceded Harry with refined indifference. 'It did nothing but rain at Christmas.'

Caroline's heart thudded. 'You were there at Christmas?'

'Oh, Matt and I had a thing going back then—nothing serious.'

Nothing serious—and yet you have to behave like strangers when I'm around. But she had found out enough—she couldn't bear to probe any deeper. She walked back to her desk, her head held rather stiffly erect. 'Well, I'd better be going—I'm in court this morning.'

'Oh, so am I,' responded Harry in that faintly patronising tone that always set Caroline's teeth on edge. 'Sir Arthur and I are in Court One—we're defending one of the Chiswick Four.'

Caroline smiled wryly to herself. She should have known. The Chiswick Conspiracy was a real headline grabber, with its undertones of political intrigue. She gave up trying to compete, and turned her attention to checking that she had all the papers she was going to need for her own case.

The case was an intriguing one, with a good deal of technical evidence that really kept her on her toes. When she won, she was very nearly as pleased as her client. Her opponent, Sir Edward Cummins, QC, congratulated her warmly, and invited her up to his Chambers for a celebratory sherry.

He was a charming man, one of the most experienced criminal lawyers at the Bar, and she was eager to hear his analysis of that and other fascinating cases. It was getting dark when she finally left him, and she didn't bother to stop off at her own Chambers, but hurried straight to catch the Tube home—Tina would have put Vicky to bed, but she should still be in time to kiss her goodnight.

She let herself into the flat quietly, and went straight into the nursery to check that all was well. Tina had forgotten the nightlight, and she switched it on, in case the child should wake. Vicky was fast asleep, snuggled down beneath her Peter Rabbit quilt, her long, dark lashes shadowing her rosy cheeks.

Caroline put a kiss on her fingertips and placed it on one shining gold curl. 'Night-night, darling,' she whispered. 'Sleep tight.' She crept from the room, pulling the door shut carefully behind her, and went across to the sitting-room.

On the threshold she paused in blank astonishment. Matt was sitting on her settee, his briefcase open beside him, reading through some papers. He glanced up, his eyes cold. 'Well, so you finally came home,' he observed curtly. 'What time do you call this?'

'What are you doing here?' she demanded, stunned.

'Minding Vicky.'

'But. . .where's Tina?'

'She's gone.'

She stared at him blankly. 'Gone? Gone where? And what business is it of yours? You've no right to interfere!'

'She's gone back to Switzerland,' he interrupted, his voice terse with annoyance. 'Her mother's been taken ill. She rang you this morning. Fortunately Hugh had the presence of mind to put the call through to me, and since you were in court and couldn't be interrupted, and I had no idea what plans you might have made in the event of such an emergency, I came over myself.'

Caroline let go her breath in a long sigh, struggling to regain her composure. 'Thank you,' she conceded reluctantly. 'I. . .I didn't know Hugh knew anything about it.'

'Of course he knows—so does Sir Arthur. Did you expect it to remain a secret?'

'I never told anyone.'

'Nevertheless, these things have a habit of being found out. I felt it was better to be honest, at least with those two.'

'Oh yes,' she threw at him sarcastically. 'Do be honest—heaven forbid that anything should cast a bad light on your career prospects!'

Matt returned her a cool, level look. 'If you'd agree to marry me, such awkward situations needn't arise.'

'*Don't* start that again,' she snapped tensely. She turned away from him quickly, and escaped to the kitchen. There she stood still, and drew in a few deep, steadying breaths. Maybe she had over-reacted a little—after all, she ought to be grateful to him for dealing with the crisis.

She leaned on the breakfast bar, offering an apologetic smile. 'I'm sorry,' she said sincerely. 'Thank you for coming over—really. Have you had anything to eat?'

'I fixed myself a snack a couple of hours ago, when I gave Vicky her tea.'

'Would you like something now? I've a couple of nice gammon steaks in the freezer—they won't take long in the microwave.'

He nodded, accepting the gesture in the spirit it was offered. 'Sounds like a good idea,' he agreed, tossing his papers back into the briefcase and closing the lid. 'Anything I can do to help?'

'No, it's all right, thank you—it doesn't take long. I'm sorry I was late,' she went on brightly. 'The jury came in on my case—I got an acquittal.'

'Against Cummins? Well done,' he approved.

'Thank you. He invited me for a sherry afterwards,' she added with a touch of pride.

Matt raised a sardonic eyebrow. 'Did he, indeed?' he drawled, an unpleasant note of sarcasm in his voice.

Caroline blinked at him in astonishment. 'He's a very nice, very respectable old gentleman,' she retorted sharply.

'He's just turned fifty, and he's a widower, and I know several women who think he's very attractive.'

'Oh, don't be ridiculous,' she snapped impatiently. '*Edward*?'

'Oh, it's Edward, is it? On first-name terms?'

'Yes, we are—not that it's any of your business.'

'Of course it's my business.'

'And please don't raise your voice,' she interrupted him, her voice icily calm. 'You'll wake Vicky.'

It appeared to cost him considerable effort to leash his temper. 'Very well,' he grated. 'We won't discuss the matter any further.'

Caroline retreated into the kitchen. His reaction to her spending a few innocent hours in the company of another man had startled her. But she really shouldn't be surprised that he was so possessive, she reflected wryly. As she was the mother of his child, he regarded her private life as his legitimate concern.

Well, she was *not* going to let him think he could get away with that. After all, it wasn't as if they were married.

CHAPTER TEN

THE meal was easy to prepare—the steaks took only a few minutes in the microwave, while the rice was cooking, and Caroline garnished the plate with slices of fresh peach and tender button mushrooms from a can—instant Cordon Bleu, she teased herself, resolutely refusing to let herself become agitated.

They ate more or less in silence, avoiding eye contact. The tension between them was still there; Matt was still angry—she could feel it radiating from him, like the heat from a fire, and she was afraid of what was going to happen when he let it go.

He cleared his plate, nodding with approval. 'That was very nice.'

'Would you like a coffee?' she asked, hoping he wouldn't notice that her voice was a little unsteady.

'Thank you.'

She carried the plates into the kitchen, and loaded them into the dishwasher while the coffee was filtering. Matt drew the sitting-room curtains and turned on a low lamp, filling the room with a warm glow. She poured the coffee, and carried the cups in on a tray, setting it down on the low table beside the settee.

She sat down on one of the armchairs opposite him, her nerve fibres growing more taut every moment as she waited for him to speak. He drank his coffee slowly. The only sound in the room was the muffled ticking of the clock, and the distant noise of the traffic on the main road.

At last he set down his empty cup, and she stiffened, apprehension knotting in her stomach. There was a dangerous light in his eyes, and she sensed that his patience had run out.

'Look,' he began incisively, 'it's time we put an end to this nonsense—I don't want Vicky messed around any more. You're going to marry me, whether you like it or not.'

She shook her head, trying desperately to maintain her cool façade. 'I've told you before——'

'You don't have to repeat yourself,' he interrupted her harshly. 'I've been very patient with you these past few months, tried to give you time to realise that it was the sensible thing to do, but I've waited long enough.'

'Oh?' Caroline heard her voice rising on the edge of hysteria. 'And how do you propose to gain my consent? Or were you thinking of a shotgun wedding? Only you've got it the wrong way round, you know—it's supposed to be the groom who has to be dragged to the altar, not the bride.'

Matt's eyes darkened with fury, and she realised with a stab of horror that she had goaded him too far. 'I'm wasting my time trying to talk sense to you,' he growled. 'There's only one way to get through to you.' He crossed the room in two strides, and before she had realised what he was going to do he had grabbed her wrists and jerked her roughly to her feet. 'I should have done this a long time ago!'

For a moment she was so startled that she couldn't do anything to defend herself. His fingers caught in the neat coil of hair at the nape of her neck, dragging her head back, and his mouth closed ruthlessly on hers, crushing her lips apart.

All the anger he had stored up for the past three years was in that kiss. He was using pure brute strength to impose his will on hers, and for one wild, glorious moment she felt herself helpless in his embrace.

But she wasn't helpless, she reminded herself angrily. She shouldn't be giving in to him like this. She tensed, struggling to push him away, and he laughed, low in his throat. 'Oh, no, you don't,' he murmured, a soft menace in his voice. 'You've held me at arm's length long enough, with your ice-cool ways. But I know just how to melt the ice, don't I?'

He bent his head to find unerringly the tiny, sensitive spot just behind her ear, teasing it with the hot, moist tip of his tongue. She held herself rigid, fighting with every ounce of will-power she possessed to resist the languid tide of desire that threatened to engulf her.

'How many times have I told you not to wear your hair like this for me?' he growled, deftly disposing of the pins and scattering them on the floor as her hair fell in a heavy wave down her back. Her protest turned into a strangled sob as he began to dust butterfly kisses down the vulnerable column of her neck, deftly unfastening the top buttons of her crisp white blouse to burrow into the shadowy hollows of her throat, his breath like fire on her skin.

'Matt, please. . .' she begged in a desperate whisper, trying ineffectually to stay his hands as they swiftly unfastened the rest of her buttons. 'We have to talk.'

'The time for talking's over,' he growled. 'You lost the case.'

With an impatient tug he dragged her blouse out of the waistband of her skirt, pulling it open at the front to uncover the ripe curves of her breasts, hiding in the delicate lacy cups of her bra. His eyes glittered in fierce possessiveness as he surveyed her.

She drew in a sharp breath, held prisoner by the intensity of his gaze. She was afraid of what was going to happen, but she had no thought of trying to escape. This moment had been inevitable for weeks.

His arms wrapped around her again, his hands sliding up over her bare back as he curved her pliant body hard against him, almost crushing the breath out of her. His mouth claimed hers again, parting her lips in hungry demand. He was ruthlessly destroying her paper-thin defences, his sensuous tongue plundering deep into the most sensitive corners of her mouth.

She closed her eyes, shamed by the ease of her surrender. He had only to touch her. . .And yet he was in full control of himself, enslaving her with a cool deliberation that scared her. There seemed to be nothing she could do to defend herself as he slid her shirt back off her shoulders and discarded it somewhere on the floor. Her bra followed it, leaving her breasts naked, the exquisitely sensitised buds of her nipples tingling as they brushed against his hard chest.

His hands slid slowly down to mould intimately over the base of her spine, and a shimmer of heat ran through her as she recognised the insistence of that hard embrace. The alarm bells were ringing in her head, but her own hunger had woken inside her, and she was powerless to resist when he scooped her up in his arms and carried her into the bedroom.

Matt pushed the door shut behind him, and set her on her feet, turning her roughly to face her own reflection in the bronze-mirrored doors of the built-in wardrobe.

'Look at yourself,' he taunted, his voice huskily soft. 'What do you see? Is that a prude, a frigid Iron Maiden? I don't think so.'

Caroline stared in shock at the image she saw through the smoky shadows in her brain. She was half naked, her skin softly flushed in contrast to the hard, weathered hands that were imprisoning her. Her lips were bruised with his kisses, her breasts as round and firm as ripe peaches, the pink nipples pert and inviting.

He let his hands slide round to cup her breasts, caressing them as she gazed into the mirror. 'You can't deny it, can you?' he mocked, a glint of triumph in his steel-blue eyes. 'You're going to do whatever I want you to do.'

She closed her eyes in defeat, that picture etching itself indelibly into her brain. His mouth was in the hollow of her throat again, the hot tip of his tongue tracing tiny circles over her skin. She leaned back against him weakly, surrendering to his insolent embrace.

He drew her back to the bed, tipping her down

on to it, his weight heavy beside her as he lay down with her, gathering her up in his arms again. His tantalising kisses tasted her shoulders, her neck, her face, finding the fluttering pulse beneath the fine skin of her temple, brushing the delicacy of her trembling eyelids.

Her mouth sought blindly for his, her lips parted hungrily to welcome his kiss. He took all that she offered, his plundering tongue swirling languorously over the sensitive inner membranes, tempting her far out of her depth. His hands were caressing her with slow, warm sensuality; she was barely aware that he was stripping off the rest of her clothes, until she lay naked in his arms.

'There,' he murmured, a note of satisfaction in his voice as he let his eyes linger over her soft, ripe curves. She flickered an apprehensive glance at his face, daunted by the primeval male hunger she saw there as his hand smoothed over her body, asserting ownership of every inch.

But his touch was stirring a fever inside her that she knew was communicating itself to him through the heat of her bare flesh, fuelling the dangerous fires of arousal in him. A low moan broke from her lips, and she moved beneath his hand in wanton invitation.

He laughed mockingly into her misted eyes. 'What's the rush?' he taunted. 'Is that the way your California beach-boys taught you to make love? Wham, bam, thank you, ma'am?'

'No,' she protested on a sobbing breath.

'No?' A dark fire was burning in his eyes. 'So, tell me about them,' he demanded, his voice low with menace. 'How many were there?'

'Dozens!' she spat at him angrily.

He caught her wrists, pinning them back on the pillow beside her head. 'You told me one or two,' he grated between clenched teeth. 'I want the truth. How many were there?'

She stared up into his eyes, unable to withstand the sheer force of his will. 'There weren't any,' she confessed, defeated. 'None at all.'

A slow smile curved his arrogant mouth. 'Good,' he murmured. 'I don't like sharing.'

His mouth came down to claim hers again, his tongue flickering between her trembling lips, inciting a response she couldn't control. His hand was fondling her breast, rolling the taut, tender nipple beneath his palm. She wrapped her arms around him, drawing him down to her.

She wanted him, without thought or shame. The hunger that had awoken inside her had driven all rational thought from her brain. Somehow, without breaking away from her, he had managed to shed his own clothes, until they lay naked together, locked in a compulsive embrace, male and female meeting as equals in desire.

All the instincts of Eve were awakening inside her, inspiring her imagination, teaching her where to touch him, how to hold him, how to arouse him as skilfully as he was arousing her. Her whole body was awash with sensation as she abandoned herself to the pure sensual delights of the erotic world he was leading her into.

His hot mouth was exploring every inch of her body, his tongue tracing tiny circles over her soft skin as he trailed a path of fire down the vulnerable column of her throat to plunder the aching swell of her breasts. She heard herself moaning softly as his lips and teeth tormented her with pleasure, nibbling and suckling the tender buds of her nipples until each was so exquisitely sensitised that every touch darted sparks of incandescent flame along her finely drawn nerve fibres.

She was melting in a sensual response, all else forgotten but what Matt was doing to her. He had moved on, over the peach-smooth curve of her stomach to rediscover the sensitive dimple of her navel. 'Mmm—hello again, sexy,' he murmured to it, blowing a warm breath into it and making her shiver with delight.

And then he moved on, running his hands up between her slim thighs to coax them apart. She yielded, lying back on the bed as he sought the most intimate of caresses. This was a sweetness beyond all her wildest dreams. She was lost in the magic he was weaving as his clever fingers found the secret nub of pleasure hidden deep within the velvet folds, and teased it with the gentlest touch, lifting the tense excitement inside her until she was crying out, begging him incoherently to take her.

And then he did, possessing her with a fierce male demand that swamped her, engulfed her, penetrated deep into the very heart of her. A tide of pure feminine submissiveness flooded through her, and she wrapped her arms around him, her spine arching to meet the hardness of his body, driven by his urgent rhythm, burning in a fire so hot that she was melting, drowning in wave after wave of molten gold, reaching up desperately to grasp at some impossible peak of pleasure. . .until a sudden shaft of white lightning pierced her brain, and she was falling, falling, to find herself tangled up with Matt and the bed-sheets, slaked and exhausted, crushed beneath his weight as the thundering beat of their two hearts returned slowly to normal.

At last he lifted his head, and looked down into her eyes. At that moment she would have done anything he wanted, walked barefoot and naked to the North Pole if that was what he asked. But he didn't say anything. He just smiled with slow satisfaction, recognising her surrender, and then he shifted his weight to lie beside her, nestling her into his arms.

'We'll talk in the morning,' he murmured.

Caroline closed her eyes, her head heavy against his shoulder, her body aching and replete. He had won, and there was no escape for her. She had always known he would win in the end.

She woke early. As the waves of sleep rolled back, she remembered what had happened in the night, and stared at the man beside her in a kind of numb horror. What had she done? She must have been mad! Cautiously she slid out of bed and tiptoed from the room, hooking her cotton dressing-gown down from the back of the door as she passed.

She went into the bathroom and bolted the door, and wrapping the dressing-gown around her naked body she sat down on the edge of the bath. There was a deep, warm ache inside her, and her breasts still felt tender from his touch. What sort of magic did that man possess? She had given in without a fight.

A wave of humiliation flooded through her. All her good resolutions had vanished like smoke in the wind—even though she had known it was no more than a calculated ploy to make her agree to marry him. A single tear spilled from the corner of her eye, and trickled down her cheek. She loved him so much, it hurt.

But she couldn't give in, even now. She stood up, gripping the edge of the sink with clenched fingers as she stared at her face in the mirror. Her eyes had a bewitched luminosity. Angrily she shook her head. No, she wouldn't give in.

A quick splash of cold water over her face made her feel a little better. There was only one thing to do—she had to go back to America. It was a drastic course of action, to give up her career entirely, to leave her friends. But it was the only thing she could do. If she stayed, Matt would continue to harass her, and in the end he would win.

She crept back into the bedroom to collect some clean clothes for the day—she was in the Old Bailey again, defending a big fraud charge. Matt still slept, sprawled naked across her bed, his face hidden in the pillow. For a long moment she gazed at him, letting her eyes linger hungrily over the powerful breadth of his shoulders, the long cleft of his spine. He looked almost. . .vulnerable in sleep, and she ached to reach out and touch him. She would never see him like this again.

But he stirred, and mumbled something in his sleep, and she snatched her clothes out of the wardrobe and fled back to the safety of the locked bathroom. There she dressed, and put up her hair into its usual severe style. With her glasses on, she felt a little safer.

She opened the door, and stopped dead. Matt was in the doorway of her bedroom, zipping up his trousers. 'Good morning,' he greeted her, his voice still husky with the memory of last night. 'You're up very early.'

'I'm in court again,' she told him briskly. 'And I was so tied up in my other case last week that I haven't had a chance to have a proper look through the papers.'

He caught her hand as she tried to move past him, and drew her into his arms. 'Tell them you need an adjournment,' he suggested, bending his head to kiss her. 'We've got wedding plans to make.'

'No.' She turned her head aside, leaning away from him.

A flicker of surprise crossed his face. 'What do you mean, no?' he rasped. 'What about last night? Don't try telling me you were drunk this time— not on Cummins' sherry.'

'I wasn't drunk,' she responded stiffly. 'But just because. . .you know how to press all the right buttons. . .I don't regard that as a very good basis for a marriage.'

He laughed mockingly. 'Don't you? I reckon it would make a pretty good start.'

She pushed her hands against his chest, trying to break his hold on her. 'Just go away,' she protested. 'Leave me alone.'

'No,' he growled forcefully. 'I know you want me. You can deny it all you like—your body gives you away every time.' His hard hands were moulding over the base of her spine, curving her hard against him, and she could feel herself responding to the fierce male pride in him. 'Why go on fighting it?' he coaxed. 'Marry me.'

'No.' She could feel the tears rising inside her, and somehow found the strength to break away from him.

'Why not?' he demanded, a jagged edge of anger in his voice.

'Because. . .oh, you know why not.' The tears spilled over. 'Because you don't really want me. I don't want you to marry me just because of Vicky.' She turned away from him, scrubbing the back of her hand impatiently across her eyes. Damn, why did she have to *cry*? 'Go away, leave me alone,' she sobbed, helpless as he drew her back into his arms again. 'Haven't you done me enough harm?'

'I love you, Caro,' he murmured urgently.

Angrily she began to struggle free of him again. 'Don't,' she pleaded. 'Don't say things like that!'

'It's true,' he insisted, his voice low and rough. 'I love you. I've loved you for a long time.'

Caroline laughed bitterly, staring up at him in disbelief. 'Oh? And what about Harry?' she challenged. 'Don't try to deny it—she told me herself. You had a thing going.'

He wouldn't let her break from his arms again, subduing her resistance with a fractional exertion of his superior strength. 'I'm not denying it,' he said, a strange, compelling force in his voice. 'When you went away I suppose I was just trying to drown out your memory. But it didn't work,' he breathed, burying his face in her hair. 'I couldn't forget you. Your long silky hair, your soft skin. . .you've haunted me, Caro.'

This time he let her go when she pulled away from him. She stood staring at him, still not ready to believe what he was saying. 'OK, if you love me, why haven't you told me before?' she demanded suspiciously.

He smiled wryly. 'I didn't know how to. Pretty funny, isn't it? I'm never at a loss for words in court, but somehow I couldn't bring myself to say those three little words to you.' He thrust his hands deep into his pockets, and stared down at the carpet, tracing its pattern with his foot. 'I had my pride. I'd never been hurt by a woman before, but when you ran out on me in Cannes. . .and then you told me it had only happened because you were drunk. . .'

He ran his hand back through his hair, and lifted his eyes to meet hers. 'I didn't know if it was true, but the fact that you could have said it. . .But I still wanted you, I wanted to make you pay, I wanted to break you until you were bleeding with love for me. I began to hope that I'd got you pregnant, so that you'd have to marry me, and oh, then I'd have got my revenge.'

'That was what I was afraid of,' she admitted in a small voice.

He shook his head. 'When I found out that there really was a baby. . .it was such a shock. I wanted to look after you then, cherish you. I knew that you couldn't really want an abortion, that it was only out of desperation. It was my one chance to put everything right between us—but I blew it.'

He smiled wryly. 'Maybe if you hadn't been so important to me. . .'

He reached for her, but she stepped back, her eyes still suspicious. 'It didn't seem that I was that important to you in Cannes,' she reminded him tartly. 'You seemed to spend most of your time chasing after that blonde.'

Matt's eyes glinted with self-mocking humour. 'Oh, yes, her. I know—I kept telling myself I should go for her. She was more than willing, and you were treating me like something the cat had dragged in. That was when I knew it was something serious. I'd only gone there on the off-chance of bumping into you—I hate the place, especially when it's crowded.'

It was her turn to stare at the carpet. 'I don't know whether to believe you,' she murmured, shaking her head. 'You and Harry. . .every time you're in the same room together, I can sense it between you.'

He laughed bitterly, moving over to take her in his arms again. 'Harry was a big mistake,' he told her gently. 'I should never have got involved with her—she didn't want to let go. Fortunately she'll be leaving us soon—she's decided politics is more her forte, and she's suckered some poor MP into taking her on as a research assistant. And there'll be no more Harrys, no more. . .what was her name, that girl in Cannes?'

'Anthea.'

'I won't be like your father, Caro,' he promised, kissing the dampness from her eyelids. 'I've sown my wild oats. From now on, it'll just be you for me. Say you love me. You seemed to be saying it last night, when we were making love, but I couldn't be sure it would mean anything after it was over. I want to hear you say it. Please.'

There was a deep note of sincerity in his voice, but still she hesitated—the words had been held in check for so long, she didn't know how to say them.

He nuzzled against her ear. 'Come on,' he coaxed gently, 'it isn't difficult, once you get used to it. Repeat after me. "I".'

'I.'

'"Love".'

On a sudden rush of happiness she capitulated, and wrapped her arms around his neck, hugging him fiercely. 'I love you,' she confessed willingly. 'I've loved you for years—before you ever even noticed I existed.'

Matt chuckled with laughter. 'I noticed you the first time I saw you,' he contradicted her, hugging her close. 'You intrigued me—I could feel that sexuality, radiating from you like the heat from a fire, and yet you seemed to deny it, to cover it up. I thought of trying to find out if I was right, but you were so chilly, I was afraid I'd get frostbite.' He swung her up in the air. 'But the days of the prudish Miss Kosek are over forever,' he warned her, a lilt of laughter in his voice. 'Mrs Farrar-Reid is never going to be allowed to be cold.'

Caroline laughed too, confident now. 'I'll still be Miss Kosek at work,' she reminded him. 'I'm going to carry on working,' she added, suddenly serious.

'You can be a High Court judge if you like,' he agreed readily. 'So long as you don't mind being the only pregnant High Court judge on the circuit.'

'I wouldn't. . .Oh, heavens, that reminds me, I'm supposed to be in court this morning! I've got to get Vicky to nursery. . .' She glanced quickly at her watch. 'I'll never have time—I haven't even got her up yet, let alone breakfast. And I'm going to have to get in touch with the agency about another girl.'

Matt caught her as she began to rush frantically around. 'Hey, calm down! I've got paperwork to do today, so I can look after Vicky. And I'm going to hire a proper, professional nanny for her. No arguments,' he insisted as she opened her mouth to protest. 'Now, you sit down and go over your case, while I get the breakfast.'

'Are you sure?' she asked doubtfully.

'Of course I'm sure. If we're both going to be working parents, we need a little teamwork. Today I can stay home, another time you'll be able to. Vicky needn't suffer, and neither will your career—I know how important it is to you. And if you *do* make it to High Court judge I shall be extremely proud of you.'

'Thank you.' She smiled shyly. 'I. . .I still can't quite believe it,' she confessed. 'It all seems like. . .some impossible dream.'

'Well, maybe this will convince you.' He wrapped her in his arms, and his mouth closed over hers in a kiss that threatened to drive all thoughts of poor Mr Goodridge's fraud case completely out of her mind.

The case went very well—after a morning of legal submissions, the prosecution agreed to drop most of the charges. Caroline's client agreed to plead guilty to two of the others, and a third was to remain on the file. By two o'clock the case was over, and her client was shaking her hand and thanking her profusely.

'I can't tell you what a relief it is that it's all over. I've been so worried! I knew it was a stupid thing to do, but it really did start off as a mistake at first—those VAT regulations are so complicated. Then, when I realised what had happened. . .well, it just seemed easier to carry on with it.'

Caroline nodded understandingly. The poor man was basically an honest person, who had been offered the temptation of making a little bit of extra money in a way he could probably almost convince himself wasn't illegal. She had felt quite sorry for him.

'Well, I can assure you of one thing—it certainly won't happen again,' he burbled on. 'One experience of that was quite enough for one lifetime!'

Over his shoulder, a familiar movement caught Caroline's eye. Matt was coming towards her, Vicky in his arms. He must have been home to change, because he was casually dressed in navy trousers and a light blue jumper—glaringly incongruous where everyone else was sombrely wearing their best clothes.

Vicky saw her, and laughed with delight. 'Mummy!' she called, holding out her arms.

Caroline smiled wryly. 'Excuse me,' she murmured to her client. 'What are you doing here?' she added quietly to Matt, taking the child from him.

'We came to meet you. Hugh said you'd probably be out by early afternoon, so I thought it would be a good opportunity to get a few things sorted out.'

'Well, yes, but. . .' She glanced around anxiously, checking that there was no one to notice the three of them together and start gossip. Her client was still standing there, and she introduced him awkwardly. 'Oh, Mr Goodridge—this is my. . .'

'Husband,' supplied Matt smoothly, shaking his hand.

Mr Goodridge's face broke into a wide smile. 'Ah! I'm very pleased to meet you, Mr Kosek. I really have cause to be very grateful to your wife— she's just rescued me from the consequences of my own folly. Have you ever had to do VAT returns? You wouldn't believe the muddle it's possible to get into!'

'Quite,' agreed Matt, at his most urbane. 'Well, if you're ready now, darling, we'd better hurry. We've a lot to do this afternoon.'

'Of course. Goodbye, Mr Goodridge—and good luck with the shops.' Caroline left him to the care of the clerk from his solicitor's, and turned to walk with Matt towards the lift. 'Vicky, don't pull Mummy's wig off, there's a good girl.' She smiled up at Matt. 'Thank you for stepping into the breach,' she said. 'I didn't quite know what to call you— anyone can see just by looking at her that Vicky's your daughter. It's a good job there aren't many people here today.'

'What does it matter?' he countered, slipping a possessive arm around her shoulders as they stepped into the lift. 'Mind you, I don't think I'd like to be called Mr Kosek all the time. It's a good job I'm taking silk—I wouldn't want your career to get too far ahead of mine.'

'You're taking silk?' she repeated, her eyes widening in delight. 'When did you hear?'

'Yesterday. I was going to tell you last night, but there seemed to be more important things to discuss.'

She couldn't restrain herself from hugging him. 'Oh. . .oh, I'm so pleased for you! It's marvellous!'

'And speaking of more important things, I hope you're going to agree to our getting married in Suffolk. I've rung my father—he's absolutely delighted, and they all send their love. We'd better send telegrams to your parents—I hope they can get over here at short notice.'

'How short?'

'Three weeks? There didn't seem to be any point in hanging around.'

'No, I suppose not,' she agreed happily, smiling up at him.

'You don't mind marrying me so soon?'

'I'll marry you anywhere and any time you choose,' she assured him readily.

'That's just what I wanted to hear.'

Matt put his arms around both of them, kissing Vicky's cheek and then kissing Caroline, long and lingeringly, oblivious of the fact that the doors had opened and two elderly barristers in silk gowns were waiting to get into the lift. After a moment one of them coughed discreetly. Caroline broke away, her cheeks flaming scarlet. They stepped out of the lift, and their senior colleagues stepped into it.

'Wasn't that Farrar-Reid, and the young woman

from his Chambers?' the younger of the two
enquired.

'I dare say,' the older responded in censorious
tones. 'You'd never have had that sort of thing in
my young day. Still,' he added with weary resignation, 'I suppose that's what comes of letting
women into the profession.'

Harlequin Presents®

Coming Next Month

Available in April wherever paperback books are sold, or through Harlequin Reader Service:

In the U.S.
P.O. Box 1397
Buffalo, N.Y.
14240-1397

In Canada
P.O. Box 603
Fort Erie, Ontario
L2A 5X3

Coming soon
to an easy chair near you.

FIRST CLASS is Harlequin's armchair travel plan for the incurably romantic. You'll visit a different dreamy destination every month from January through December without ever packing a bag. No jet lag, no expensive air fares and *no* lost luggage. Just First Class Harlequin Romance reading, featuring exotic settings from Tasmania to Thailand, from Egypt to Australia, and more.

FIRST CLASS romantic excursions guaranteed! Start your world tour in January. Look for the special **FIRST CLASS** destination on selected Harlequin Romance titles—there's a new one every month.

NEXT DESTINATION:
GREECE

 Harlequin Books

JTR4

Take 4 bestselling love stories FREE

Plus get a FREE surprise gift!

Special Limited-time Offer

Harlequin Reader Service®

Mail to

In the U.S.
3010 Walden Avenue
P.O. Box 1867
Buffalo, N.Y. 14269-1867

In Canada
P.O. Box 609
Fort Erie, Ontario
L2A 5X3

YES! Please send me 4 free Harlequin Presents® novels and my free surprise gift. Then send me 6 brand-new novels every month, which I will receive months before they appear in bookstores. Bill me at the low price of $2.24* each—a savings of 51¢ apiece off cover prices. There are no shipping, handling or other hidden costs. I understand that accepting the books and gift places me under no obligation ever to buy any books. I can always return a shipment and cancel at any time. Even if I never buy another book from Harlequin, the 4 free books and the surprise gift are mine to keep forever.

*Offer slightly different in Canada—$2.24 per book plus 69¢ per shipment for delivery. Sales tax applicable in N.Y. Canadian residents add applicable federal and provincial taxes.

106 BPA CAP7 (US)   306 BPA U103 (CAN)

Name _____
                                    (PLEASE PRINT)

Address _____ Apt. No. _____

City _____ State/Prov. _____ Zip/Postal Code _____

This offer is limited to one order per household and not valid to present Harlequin Presents® subscribers. Terms and prices are subject to change.

PRES-BPA1DR   © 1990 Harlequin Enterprises Limited

COMING IN 1991 FROM HARLEQUIN SUPERROMANCE:

Three abandoned orphans,
one missing heiress!

Dying millionaire Owen Byrnside receives an
anonymous letter informing him that twenty-six years
ago, his son, Christopher, fathered a daughter. The
infant was abandoned at a foundling home that
subsequently burned to the ground, destroying all
records. Three young women could be Owen's long-
lost granddaughter, and Owen is determined to track
down each of them! Read their stories in

#434 HIGH STAKES (available January 1991)
#438 DARK WATERS (available February 1991)
#442 BRIGHT SECRETS (available March 1991)

Three exciting stories of intrigue and romance by
veteran Superromance author Jane Silverwood.